AB TERRA 2020

— AB TERRA 2020 —

EDITED BY YEN OOI • • •

CONTENTS

2020 HAS BEEN SUCH A YEAR THAT A VAST NUMBER OF US ON EARTH SUFFERED FROM ONE THING OR ANOTHER: COVID-19, MOUNTAIN FIRE, LOCUST PLAGUE, volcano eruption, trade conflict, racism, rape, rumors…Things that we thought would only take place in science fiction stories took place every day in the world surrounding us and are still going on. Many science fiction writers find it hard to write when reality feels more science fiction than science fiction itself. We are not sure what the future will be like. We are not even sure whether there will be a future. We hope that what has been happening is not real and that the year 2020 can be reloaded from the very beginning. Facing such enormous unease and uncertainty, some people find it difficult to care about things that take place beyond their horizon, let alone in an imaginary world. What, then, is the meaning of reading or writing science fiction in 2020?

First, science fiction portrays possible or alternative futures. Via reading and writing science fiction, we speculate about and predict futures, which can be both good and bad. The good futures may serve as guidance, while the bad futures may ring alarm bells for us. Although 2020 has disturbed our predictions about the future, we can still see from science fiction that there are millions of possibilities, and we—every one of us on the Earth—may shape the future we want to live in, together. It is a hard and long process, but science fiction serves as the lighthouse in the darkness, guiding us through the night.

Second, science fiction tends to address global and universal topics, which makes it easier for a global audience to relate to. This does not mean that all science fiction tends to be the same. Instead, science fiction can be diverse in representation of culture, gender, and sexuality, both physical and neurodiversity, and much more. It is about how people react to and interact with global and universal changes or challenges. Combining these diverse perspectives, we obtain a viewpoint that is beyond any single group on Earth, an *ab terra* view.

Third, reading and writing science fiction cultivates the ability to imagine and to empathize, which is vital in this era. Science fiction stories are about imaginary characters in imaginary worlds. To appreciate them, you need to imagine things that you have never seen or experienced and to empathize with characters that are completely different from you. Your brain needs to adapt to unfamiliar characteristics to allow you to enjoy the story. If you are able to comprehend imaginary characters and worlds, you will also be able to comprehend what is happening to other people in other places on this planet, feeling their pain and understanding their struggles. Through reading and writing science fiction, we may learn to be more patient and considerate about others, making the world a better place.

Luckily, 2020 also brought good news: NASA shared an update on its Artemis program, which plans to land the first woman and the next man on the Moon in 2024; Chang'e 5, which will bring lunar soil and rock samples back to Earth, is scheduled for launch in November 2020; and Mars missions from the UAE, China, and the United States have all been successfully launched in 2020. We start from Earth, and we go beyond the Earth. And more important, the next groups to step on the Moon or on Mars will be made of both men and women, of people from diverse backgrounds, from different countries and cultures, but all from *terra*. Although controversies will still exist on Earth, explorations require collaboration and mutual understanding, and science fiction has its role here.

Ab Terra 2020 showcases twelve science fiction short stories with diverse cultural perspectives but which share a similar feeling of looking back at our world. In these stories, we can see conflicts and communication, fear and hope, as well as memories and the future. We can see that the authors have used their imaginations and empathy to write stories that may echo to all. The anthology provides a way to perceive our reality via alternative realities. While these stories may not influence our world in a direct and fast way, they are seeds. Given sunshine, water, air, and time, they may grow and make our world a better place.

It is great to know that *Ab Terra 2020* is only the beginning of a series of amazing projects. The journey from Earth has just begun.

Regina Kanyu Wang
Shanghai, October 2020

– AB TERRA 2020 –

ICHIRI - BY CLARE MCNAMEE-ANNETT

JÈKU CANARA. SIMPLY, "HOME OF THE PEOPLE." HAVE YOU SEEN IT FROM ONE HUNDRED KILS ABOVE IN AN ERA-JU—A *spacecraft*? PALE PINK NOW. THE COLOR of our blood. My planet is within the congregation of star systems you know as Andromeda. It is tied to your planet by the shared fate of conquest. You, conqueror; us, conquered. Many Jèku Caran still hope for salvation. I taste it in the water, in the settling tidal pools (the tarry pitch of hope, sick-sweet as sea-char, insubstantial), but the truth of our civilization's impending decimation is calculable. Following the statistical curve of Jèku Caran deaths since invasion, our people have three ren years left on our planet. You, conqueror; us, conquered. Thus, we are bound to each other.

The Jèku Caran have no *mouths*, no *tongues*; our ears exist within our minds. Did you know this? Did you know that our skin and tentacles, slick with the conductivity of lipid-rich oligodendrocytes, simply reverberate the voices of each other's thoughts? You call it *echo*. This is the cousin of the word. We think and others hear without *speaking*. Our communication has confused your kin for years.

When your ancestors were emerging from the sea, Jèku Caran were self-aware. We farmed diverse fields of sea-flora; we bred invertebrates. By the time your species was bipedal, Jèku Caran piloted Era-ju into orbit and learned the rudimentary secrets of bending time. I would not expect you to understand. It takes the human a mere two hundred sixty-five Earth days to gestate: such a short amount of time for the body to begin. Human: species of death and invasion. Species of conquest and decimation. A species that developed the means of atom-combustion, of space-travel, of decade-long food preservation, but remains underdeveloped in the wisdom that war begets loss begets war. As such I would not expect you to understand.

o

Five people. One mission. Bend time within the sphere, says Alan-ju. *Emerge in the critical moment. You know the coordinates of their planet. You know what is at stake.* His tentacles are brown from years of battle. His luminous eye looks into each of ours in turn. When he looks into mine, I close my mind to him. The thoughts of the people are loud, and the war wages above our enclave. We have come underneath the skin of the earth, where the spacecrafts are built and sold.

The civilization of the people is upon your arms, says Ca-len. *May your reach be long; may you strike swiftly.* The two Jèku stand before us, last of the council. It is a small enclave, by necessity secreted beneath the open waters. Standing before Alan-ju and Ca-len, there are five of us. Lana-klee, commander; Ellis-ren, bender of time. Su-ylen the mathematician and Qi-raw the soldier. And I, Ku. I am their pilot.

The sadness-turned-anger in Ca-len's voice is unmistakable. In our tradition this engenders shame. The Jèku abhor anger, vengeance, lust for pain: all emotions begotten from loss. Fifty ren years ago, any Jèku with such emotions would bury her face and banish her body to the edges of the city so her feelings, like poison, wouldn't corrupt the health of the people. But today, these emotions are as tangible as stone, as ubiquitous as sand-lice. War changes the very culture of our nation.

We will strike swiftly, replies Lana-klee, *for the hope of our homeland. For our dead.*

With their farewell, the five of us board the Era-ju. I take my seat at the helm. I ignite the ship.

The Era-ju is a perfect sphere within an arrow. Beneath me splitting atoms ignite in a controlled eruption no living body has seen. The pulse of it is known but imperceptible. The pistons whine, and our sudden velocity floors all five of us, each strapped into the ship's interior walls with dried sea vines and distilled gelatinous sap. Beside me I see Ellis-ren's tentacles cradling his face despite the force.

Soon the speed of our ship overtakes our planet's pull. We leave our homeland for Earth.

o

Whom are you leaving behind, sister? LANA-KLEE ASKS me.

My bor-an, may she rest in water, I reply.

o

CHILDREN ARE RAISED IN THE NURSERY POOLS, EACH Jèku eager to swim into the ren light. Ren: our singular star. Unlike our neighbors, she gives light without an orbiting twin. When I was in infancy, I believed Ren was lonely. Our star was abstraction only: an image gifted to me by the wisdom of adult Jèku, who passed its warmth through my skin, formless and strange.

Jèku young never see ren light. As newborns, our skin is too sensitive to withstand the heat; every thought-sound-emotion we perceive through our skin is magnified, garbled, a strange and nonsensical barrage. As children, we spend our days growing, learning to speak and listen, absorbing the knowledge of ancestors. We watch the bodies of adult Jèku drift at the ocean's surface, above us. Adult Jèku prefer to live in water but are not bound to it. We can roam in air, in dry heat, until moisture leaves our skin.

It takes the blood and spirits of many Jèku to merge to make one child. As Jèku, we gestate for years.

Before the death at Ara-cannes, I was known as Ich-iri. In the warm waters of our nursery pools, I grew beside one other Jèku. Her name was Ku-glen. As we formed, our tentacles became wrapped around each other: a rare circumstance, a symmetry reflecting the practice of love among older Jèku. Though not kin, we were called twins, or *bor-an*: the name for two stars circling each other within a galaxy.

I am a strange Jèku. I was born with the gift and curse of silence. I can close my skin's voice to others when I choose. What can this mean? All my life, for no known reason, I have been able to choose to keep my thoughts silent. My feelings can be hidden from others. My skin can be mute; it has been said I am built of stone instead of water. It is a rare and unnatural ability. No Jèku understands the reason, nor why Ku-glen was the only Jèku ever able to hear my hidden thoughts. I could keep no secrets from her, may she rest in water.

○

DAYS PASS. AROUND US THE DARK OF THE GALAXY envelops our ship in passive observance.

○

Is our ship on course, sister? ASKS LANA-KLEE.

Directly, I reply, giving her the image of our trajectory as she touches my arm.

Ellis-ren will bend time at the peak of our speed, when the boundaries of space-time grow thin, she says. *Come listen to him describe the mission.*

We congregate at the Era-ju's innermost circle.

The human is named "Oleta Volkova," says Ellis-ren. She was born in Earth-year 2138. This is the history. In the twenty-second century the human planet is barely inhabitable: a receptacle of waste, bearing an overpopulated species. A dying planet. Humans are poor stewards of their land and seas. Those with power seek to escape its confines.

At the age of fifty-seven Oleta becomes responsible for the creation of the long-range spacecraft capable of reaching our congregation of stars. She merges two technologies of the time: the energy of split atoms and the rudimentary spacecraft of her people. Twenty Earth-years after this invention, human scientists conclude our star system is most similar to theirs, and our planet most habitable. An assembly of humans embark for Jèku Canara in their year 2215.

If this body, Oleta Volkova, prematurely dies, our civilization will be saved, says Lana-klee.

How can we be certain no other human body will create the vessels of conquest? asks Qi-raw.

Our sphere has calculated the statistical improbability, replies Su-ylen. *Oleta is simply unique: a savant whose rare intellect is nurtured by the specific environments of her upbringing.*

No other human is capable of its invention? says Qi-raw.

It is doubtful, says Ellis-ren.

This knowledge is unsettling.

The concept of a "savant" is a human one. Our philosophies believe in the importance of chance in the making of great discoveries and the influence of collective conditions. Why would one body matter more than another? From the cycle of time emerges similar circumstances, conditions, and means. The Jèku believe that to say that someone is "unique" is to be blind to time. Still, a singular event: the birth of this human child. Perhaps our scientists fall short. Perhaps our ancient philosophies are half-measured; perhaps our laws have been waiting a millennium to be disproven. This is war. Anything is possible.

Oleta's own son leads the first expedition to Jèku Canara, says Ellis-ren.

Our collective thoughts turn to the first landing. Jèku Caran felt the metal spaceship crash into our pale sea. Bodies of strange white shells emerged: bodies with only four short tentacles and grossly hardened skin. Silent bodies: capable of touch but not communication. Our collective memories are ripped with explosions, torn skin, and our grandmothers' bloodshed. Images we have passed down through generations.

If we end her life, we destroy both her lineage and the technology of conquest, says Lana-klee.

Never before have the Jèku intervened in the trajectory of time, says Su-ylen. *To end a life. We are faced with the magnitude, the grave significance, of this task.*

On the brink of extinction, we believe in intervention, I whisper, thinking about the human concept of irony. *And yet to kill the young is contrary to every Jèku teaching. To believe in exceptional circumstance is against the wisdom of centuries.* I say this in my hidden way, so only my *bor-an* could have heard me. Having the gift of silence offers a two-faced freedom, which may lead to insolence, independence, and rebellion.

o

Clare McNamee-Annett

KU-GLEN AND I OUTGREW THE DEEP NURSERY POOLS
at the height of the human invasion. Separately, we
enlisted in auxiliary forces for the Jèku defense. Ku-
glen left our city to train as a translator. I missed her.
I became a pilot, driving a medic ship, transporting
injured Jèku to safety.

o

YEARS AFTER LEAVING, WHEN THE WAR HAD WORN
through our naïve hope and tenacity, Ku-glen came
back to the city. She wanted to see me. Her tentacles
were stained black from her work, but her luminous
eye was still green, like mine, and brighter than I
remembered.

How does one communicate with humans? I asked
her, sitting on a hill, the Jèku capital a mass of rubble
before us.

Ku-glen told me what she had observed. Humans
we Jèku had captured created strange markings on
stone, which seemed to alert others of their location.
Over years of study, she mastered the human art of
written words, above ground, where the marks she
made with lines of black Jekka-shell ink would last
until storm-surge tides washed them away. Using her
knowledge, she offered aid in negotiations with the
invaders. Nurseries could be saved, cities could be
spared from bloodshed, if we Jèku met the invaders'

demands. *They want food, shelter, space,* she told me. *They want our villages, our ships, our tools. If we give them these things, they spare us.*

Ku-glen was important. I wasn't important. *I don't know why she came back,* I thought to myself as she spoke to me of her work.

Ku-glen heard me. She told me she was tired of the war. She missed me. She had asked to be transferred home.

Ku-glen came to live with me.

For the first time, I felt at peace with all things.

○

ONE NIGHT, WHEN OUR TENTACLES WERE WRAPPED around each other and our minds shared images of dreaming, Ku-glen spoke of a human child. This human was able to speak like the Jèku. This human could bring her thoughts to the surface and share them through her skin. What image was this? What prophecy?

I trusted Ku-glen, and her dream stopped me in my path when, transporting three injured Jèku from Ara-cannes to Jup-ter, I found the human infant wrapped in soiled leaves at the edge of the city. The infant had a red, soft face and a wide mouth that screamed a high-pitched cry. I felt the cry in my skin as I held her.

The infant's tentacles were impossibly small, with five tiny arms like small fish stretching out beyond them.

Fingers, said Ku-glen, when I took the child home.

Fingers, I said, slowly. I touched her *fingers.* They were soft, warm, dull. Delicate. Breakable. They grasped easily, curling into themselves. Each bent in three miniscule places.

Ku-glen wrapped the infant in her tentacles with tenderness. She named the child Cor-innis, which means *One whose skin has yet to speak.*

o

WHEN KU-GLEN WAS SLAIN, I BECAME KU. I LEFT MY name Ich-iri at the place where her body soaked the shore in blood. For *Ich-iri* means "joy" and the love one has for living; my name no longer belonged to me.

I stopped myself from lighting aflame the fuel from the medic ship and plummeting into the murderous humans' war-camp.

Vengeance is a lazy form of grief, said Cor-innis.

o

KU-GLEN AND I GUESSED THAT COR-INNIS CAME FROM an inland human settlement. Her progenitors were likely victims of war.

o

COR-INNIS GREW UP IN A TIME OF WAR, HIDDEN IN our home: within a network of caves, where sea meets land, at the outskirts of Ara-cannes. Ku-glen said human children need the sun, not the sea. But the sky was scorched with fire every day. It was dangerous to be outside, under the open air. We lived in the marsh-caves—half-water, half-earth—on the cusp of two worlds, on the borderlands. Cor-innis grew up collecting sea-sap, nutritive and medicinal plants from the marsh tides, and warming her dry human body against our tentacles. We spoke to her through gestures. We spoke in rudimentary emotions, transmitted through our skin. Yes, her skin could hear us, though it heard so little. Speaking to Cor-innis through her skin was like speaking across leagues of distance, or on opposite sides of thick stone.

She was unlike Jèku young. Whereas, as children, the Jèku are most receptive to knowledge, Cor-innis's skin and arms were armored. She was simple, beginning, unable to understand. As she grew, her skin became callused instead of soft and receptive like Jèku skin. But Cor-innis matured. Ku-glen and I learned that she was listening.

Cor-innis felt joy easily. She wrapped her body in sea-grass from the tide. She drew illustrations on dried stone—pictures of us and our home. She learned to draw with detail and accuracy. She had a steady hand. Ku-glen had rudimentary knowledge of human life, which we attempted to impart to Cor-innis however we were able. Together, we learned how to speak.

Humans have a word for rearing young. Humans have a word for the person you become when you are responsible for raising children. The Jèku Caran have no word for what Ku-glen and I were doing with Cor-innis. The Jèku Caran have no word for the people we were becoming. Ku-glen and I were renegades, anomalies, freaks: if Cor-innis was the enemy, we were enemy sympathizers. We both knew if we were discovered, we were bound to be punished. Harmed and shamed. Made examples of by the Jèku Assault Forces.

How can a peaceful people be so vengeful? I asked, then. *Will our principles be lost within one generation?* A broken, raging people have only the tools of war. These tools cannot heal them. War begets pain. Pain begets rage; rage begets war.

But pain may also beget other things, said Ku-glen. *And these things will change you. If you let them.*

○

COR-INNIS FOUND KU-GLEN'S BODY. I HELD HER IN my tentacles as she cried.

When humans are unable to contain their pain or joy, it runs forth from within their bodies. The first moment I saw Cor-innis cry was my first moment of understanding. *Ku-glen, why is salt water spilling from Cor-innis? Why is the ocean emerging from her eyes?*

Ku-glen touched her tentacles to Cor-innis's face, certain she was dying. In all her years, she had never seen a human cry.

Our sea, of Jèku Canara, is our beginning. We hatch and we learn in the sea. Without our nursery pools, Jèku would never grow or gain wisdom. I never understood how Cor-innis could produce the same salt waters of my homeland. When I witnessed this, I was overwhelmed by connection. I felt *em-aris*, the Jèku word for "love."

o

KU-GLEN WAS MURDERED BY TWO HUMANS WHEN SHE was collecting sweet-sap from the seashore.

o

AS I HELD COR-INNIS, I LOOKED UP INTO THE SKY. More drones were flying above us, sure to see one Jèku and one human holding each other on the shore of the ocean below. I gestured to Cor-innis to seek shelter; I screamed it into her skin. Cor-innis ran into our network of caves, mouth open, making human sounds of agony. I bent over Ku-glen. I touched her still body, her unbearable coldness. I caressed her. For the first time, I heard deafening silence. The shore around us was filling with her blood. My tentacles were slick with it, Ku-glen's blood in the sand. I wanted never to leave her. I covered her with my body, trying with all of my being to pour my life into her still form, to fill her body with my still-living spirit. Ku-glen remained cold.

In that moment, the name *Ich-iri* no longer belonged to me. I knew, as long as I lived, my spirit could no longer possess such a feeling. I took the name *Ku* in her memory. If not for Cor-innis, I would have chosen to end my life. Of this, humans have no words or understanding.

o

ABOARD THE SHIP, I AM SILENT. MY CREW TASKS ME with the responsibility of pilot, and names me words for "stoic" and "sleeping." I try not to betray my history. I have convinced them to let me come this far.

Days pass, though in space-time travel these measurements lose meaning. One simply moves from one place-time to another. One exists in the moment one harbors. Ellis-ren bends time back to the human year 2138. I steer the ship in arrival at the human Earth, its blue-green pattern sequestered by gray clouds and fume. The instant I see it, the heart of me stands still. The planet is drifting, turning, just behind the horizon of its moon. There is so much color and gas. The Earth world is so beautiful.

Even from this distant orbit, I can see that their lands are burning.

Lana-klee finds the coordinates of Oleta, the human child, and I bring our spaceship to land. On this side of the planet, the world is dark: the bright star, which burns our eyes, floats now behind this dying orb. We dress in spacesuits filled with water, but walk on their hard, dry land.

There are noises in this land. There are lights. Hard structures. The mass of their planet makes gravity heavy. We move slowly in their night.

We capture the infant from her nursery, stunning the humans who care for her with the numbing sap of sweet-char which grows in rare sea fields on Jèku Canara. It is easy to take her: she is vulnerable, defenseless. Lana-klee grasps Oleta in one spacesuit-covered tentacle. She carries the infant with awkwardness, carelessness, with no respect for the infant's need for closeness or warmth. I move behind her, watching.

I suppose she has never held a human before.

o

LANA-KLEE WILL KEEP THE INFANT IN A QUARANTINED pod. She will then shoot the pod into space after we leave orbit. She thinks this, loudly. So it is easy to hear her thoughts and know her plans.

I lift the ship off the human planet. The speed and thunder of us is hidden from Earth by Ellis-ren's wrinkle in space-time.

Then I leave the helm of Era-ju.

I have so little time.

Ku, says Qi-raw, alarmed. *You must steer the ship.*

Yes. I must steer the ship.

I reach for the tranquilizer of sweet-char and immobilize Qi-raw. I hit Ellis-ren and Su-ylen as I pass them in the circular halls. They are alive and will reawaken when the sweet-char leaves their skin. I am sorry to have hurt them.

I run fast to the quarantined pod. Lana-klee is putting the infant into it. The infant is crying, making human sounds for sadness, coldness, hunger. *Want. Need.* Cor-innis would make those sounds.

Humans are so loud, marveled Ku-glen, listening. *They expel air at such a pitch, so young.*

I push past Lana-klee. I grab the infant from the pod.

What are you doing, Ku? says Lana-klee, startled. *Why are you taking the human?*

Yes, I reply. *I am taking her.*

The human will destroy our civilization, says Lana-klee, faltering as I point the sweet-char tranquilizer at her core.

The human is a child, and has a name, I say.

You choose to betray your people, Ku. Her voice is a storm-surge tide, desperate, buffeting against the thin walls of our ship. *You hold the singular event in your arms.*

Yes, sister. I shoot Lana-klee. *I hold her.*

o

THE SUN RISES BEYOND THE HUMAN EARTH, BATHING us both in light. The light is skin-blinding pain beyond pain. I look into it. The star of the human Earth. So much smaller than Ren. So much closer. I hold the singular event in my arms: the human, whose life may lead to the inevitable destruction of my people.

Will it? I wonder. Has the future set its course, like a spaceship, in the endless sky? You, conqueror. Us, conquered. What else could be possible?

I hold her small body against my side. She is as Cor-innis was: delicate, breakable. She has dry, quiet skin. She is full of want and need; she is vulnerable.

By her choices, we are bound to each other.

I give her the gift of my memories. Ku-glen, on a ridge at Ara-cannes, her bright eye awash with our sunset: fire-orange over pale green water. The bloodshed of first contact. The terror and devastation of war. Cor-innis, as she is ripped from our cave by Jèku militants, tears mingling with the salt of the ocean, her high-pitched scream. Alien sameness, Cor-innis. My daughter.

Her skin begins to speak.

She is crying, now. I hold her closer.

Together, we hurtle through space. Back to her homeland.

COME WATER · COME NAVIGATOR - BY ELIZABETH KATE SWITAJ

Most mornings, Roberlynn woke gradually with the sunrise, but this was one of the mornings when her memories of Hawai'i jolted her awake before enough rays could gather for anyone to call it light. She pushed off her mat and rolled into the water before the memory could come into focus. Was it the white boy who drugged her on a date and dragged her back to his room in their dorm? Was it one of the assaults that were trades, or trades that were assaults, while she was living rough on the Ala Wai canal or wherever she could hide from that night's police sweep?

The water between her *walap* and the smaller *tipnol* moored closer to the floating city's permanent pontoons could not compare to the lagoons of her home islands, but that was all gone now. By the time her uncle had brought her back to Majuro to get clean, the corals had bleached, the sharks fled, and the brightest fish had been eaten. The canoes at least gave her a sheltered space to float and let the memories drain from her, the way her aunts had taught her when they gave her the drink to clean away the pregnancy.

Roberlynn rolled onto her back and took a few strokes away from her outrigger canoe, inward toward the smaller ones. In a few hours, she would go to meet with Iroij Loeak; she and the other *walap* navigators had received word of the summons just the night before. She remembered her first meeting with the chief of the floating city. Her heart had already been pounding like a King Tide on her ribs, and when he said he knew of her navigational studies, a storm surge filled her chest. That was before he took her out on his personal *korkor* and let her show him what she could do. It had been over a decade since then, and he had personally overseen her progress to leader of the *walap*, the largest of canoes. Over and over he had told her that so much of their culture had been lost in the years of colonization and capitalism that no one could really say what *manit* meant. Over and over, she had repeated what one of her Pacific Studies professors had said: that forcing a culture to freeze was one way for imperialists to kill it. She even said it on mornings like this one, when no one was there to fight her. She pulled herself back up onto her *walap* as the sky turned gold. She could smell the eggs her crew were frying for breakfast, but she never ate before these meetings.

Roberlynn pulled her shift dress—the woven pandanus piece with long slits for mobility—over her head. She began her journey to the center of the floating city by extending a plank over the water she had just swum through.

o

"I'LL KEEP THIS SHORT," SAID THE *Iroij*, SMOOTHING out the *lavalava* he had gotten from the last Polynesian sailors to visit their *weto*. The group had already gone through all the ceremony and were seated on mats inside their chief's lean-to. "The voyages to the west have returned with little to offer but news of conflict. We need more soil and new plants that can better grow contained in our city. Navigator Alson, Navigator Kyle: you've served well, but I want to send someone else east. Navigator Reimers?"

Roberlynn looked up, remembering only at the last moment to avert her eyes from the gaze of the *Iroij*. "I... I...sir?"

"You are the only of my *walap* leaders who ever lived in what used to be the United States."

"In Hawai'i, not—"

"You will guide your *walap* to what used to be California and follow the coast, at your discretion.

Find out what happened to America. Bring us any survivors who will come. Botanist Trevor and his team will join you to gather soil and cuttings." He dismissed the navigators with a nod, but Roberlynn remained.

"You have something to say, Navigator Reimers?"

"If I may?"

Another, fainter nod.

"My time in the U.S. did not go well. I'm not sure I understand them any better than any other navigator."

The *Iroij* swept his gray hair out of his eyes. His wife had refused to leave Majuro even after the first tsunami had taken advantage of the changed ocean floor to strike the atoll; it had been relatively small, taking out only a few houses, but it had carried the sound of twisting, tearing metal and left behind coppery-smelling muck. Leaving Ebeye after the full military takeover of Kwajalein, as her people before her had left Enewetak with its leaky dome of radiating waste, had already been too much for the *Leroij*. The *Iroij* had never sent a canoe back; the survivors, he said, had already come. His wife could no longer see to it that he cut his hair.

"Roberlynn"—her given name startled her into looking at his eyes—"that is precisely why you're the right choice. So many of our people always spoke of our American friends..."

"But surely after all that's happened..."

"Especially after all that's happened."

○

ROBERLYNN DIDN'T UNDERSTAND. AND SHE REPLAYED her lack of understanding over and over in her head. She didn't pause to tease the children who leapt from pontoon to pontoon and occasionally threw each other in. She didn't notice the cats weaving around her legs, though her feet expertly avoided tripping over them. She didn't hear the mating dogs or smell the drying kelp on racks. She didn't even see Tulpe until the lone Pohnpeian in the floating *weto* was kissing her lips.

Tulpe pulled back, keeping her hands on Roberlynn's shoulder. She had a full foot and least a hundred pounds on Roberlynn. "Now, what's on your mind?"

"I'm being sent on another voyage."

"How long?"

"I…don't know. Weeks? Months? It depends on what we find."

"Roberlynn, where are you going?"

"America."

Tulpe's hands dropped to her sides. Her writing hand, her left, made a fist. "You wouldn't have come to tell me." It wasn't a question.

"You would have come by the *walap*. It'll take a few days to gather supplies and the shore team."

Tulpe nodded. "And I won't see you before you leave."

"You know I have to prepare."

"And I know your crew gathers its own goods, and that you're years beyond the need to study the stick chart."

"This route is…"

"Roberlynn, I love you, and I know what you're not saying. You don't have to lie to me. You don't have to say anything."

"I…"

Tulpe's kiss before turning away fell on Roberlynn's cheek. "I'll wait, navigator, but watch out for your sailors. They become restless on these long trips."

○

MOST OF THE PEOPLE ON THE *walap* SPENT THEIR time on the open sea trying to distract themselves by reading, writing, singing, or fishing. Some, the older ones especially, still carried old phones and tablets instead of the newer solar readers. They half believed that somewhere the signal would still come through: the Internet couldn't have just vanished. The land team had a swig of fermented coconut juice, though the crew could not partake; they had to be ready to turn the sail on Roberlynn's command.

For Roberlynn, as on every journey, the sea occupied her. She flowed with currents, tides, and surges. Only the wind could intrude—never her own thoughts, never her memories. Even her dreams were water, salt, and motion. She was the ocean. The stick charts were not tools to teach patterns that you memorized: they were ways of entering the mysteries that every fish and whale already knew.

One afternoon, the feeling of eyes on the back of her neck broke her from her reverie. She turned to find Chris, her most experienced sailor, who asked her what exactly it was that a navigator did.

"It's not what I do. It's what I am."

"That doesn't make any sense."

Roberlynn shrugged, not letting herself smile. "I'm not a teacher yet, and anyway, the rest of it is oath-bound."

Chris scoffed and kicked an imaginary dog. "By *jowi?*"

"By who you show yourself to be." Roberlynn shook her head. She wasn't trying to make him angry, though that would be the best way to prove her point. "Your mother's line is only part of that."

The sailor and the navigator turned back to the water. A week later, that same water turned slate and swelled under rain and wind. Chris asked if they should take the sail in. She shook her head. He stood over the prow where she sat to breathe the wind and asked again.

"I don't want to waste this wind or drift the way the surge would take us," she shouted because now there was thunder.

"This wind is going to damage the sail."

"Are you telling me you're not prepared to mend it?"

"I am, but"—another thunderclap—"what if the wind rises and shreds the sail beyond repair?"

"Are you telling me that you didn't pack a spare?"

"I'm saying we should save that for what we can't avoid."

"The winds won't get that high." The rain, however, was biting.

"Remember this, navigator: the crew won't follow if you get it wrong." He turned and pretended to tighten a lashing.

Throughout the day and night, waves rolled over the open hull. Some of the less-seasoned passengers tied themselves down for safety, but by sunrise the system had passed, and the *walap* had lost nothing. Only one small tear appeared in the sail. Roberlynn said not to repair it.

o

SHE WAS NOT THE FIRST TO SPOT THE BIRDS THAT meant they were coming near a shore. It was Chris. "Where do you think we'll land?" he asked Roberlynn.

"Los Angeles, or whatever it has become." It had become light and shadow, shattered glass floating or tethered to remnants of towers.

Two days later, they saw one building, tipping but still holding space. Someone could still live in there. Something could survive. Rusted rebar fingers reached out of its walls into the salt spray.

"We can't go in there," said Chris. "Should we follow the coast north or south?"

"For now, we need to drift here at the edge."

"For how long?"

She shook her head. "I'll tell you when." The water had fled from her mind, and she could not force it. It would bring something new, or old, when it returned. She shivered like she had not let herself do since the rain.

Every day he came to her. Every day she told him no. On the seventh day, Botanist Trevor came as his second. On the eighth day, they were joined by three more.

"I could turn this boat around," said Chris.

"I won't navigate for you if you do."

"I could make you."

"I'd rather die than be forced to do anything by a man again."

No one spoke to Roberlynn for the next few days, though someone fixed the sail's tear. She slept less, and the water didn't come in her sleep. She wouldn't let any dreams come to her so close to America until finally she fell into a sleep deeper than she had never known before, and she stood in that shabby dorm, the rapist asleep on the bed. The water started rising, though there was no storm. She let him sleep and ran up the stairs. She reached the ceiling; the water met her soles. She dove into the currents, became a wave and then a surge. She drifted down and saw the rapist drown.

In that moment, he was every man: the ones who bought her, the ones who stole, and the good ones, too. She wasn't healed, but she could move on with the ocean inside her.

She woke to sunrise, found Chris asleep, and grasped his shoulder to wake him. "It's time to turn us north. There isn't anyone to come for us, not anymore."

"Anyone? You mean like a storm?"

"Something like the weather, yes." But he saw it all in her open, dreaming eyes.

Chris followed her command. The journey would succeed. They'd be welcomed with flowers, and Roberlynn would accept Tulpe's arms in a way she never had before—publicly, and more.

Chris would never become a navigator, though he would often try to make the water come.

CHRONOTOPE BY RAUL CIANNELLA - TRANSLATED BY RACHEL CORDASCO

In a hypothetical razor-sharp view that saw everything, there would be no 'flowing' time and the universe would be a block of past present and future. But we conscious beings live in time because we only see a faded image of the world.

—Carlo Rovelli, *Seven Short Physics Lessons*, 2014

IT HAPPENED YESTERDAY.

I was in the office, of course. I work, or rather *used to work* (I'm still not accustomed to the past tense), in a large, artificially ventilated space on the twenty-first floor of a crystal-parallelepiped building in the data entry department of DataTech. My unit is—*was*—made up of four employees (including myself) plus one unit manager: Jazz_Mina, a perfume sample collector.

Like the other forty units in our department, we were arranged frontally, two by two, along a rectangular melamine table adjacent to the floor's outer wall. One of the short sides of the table aligned almost perfectly with the sill of the open space's huge window. I don't know why I'm dwelling on these trivial details of design and architecture—perhaps because I never understood what had pushed DataTech to build a structure with such problematic windows. The excessive solar light that filtered in made it difficult, especially under clear-sky conditions, to see the monitors, in addition to producing excess heat. This was mitigated by DataTech's PEs (Productivity Experts), who always kept the blackout filter active and set the air conditioning to well below room temperature. A wasteful expedient from both an economic and an energy point of view, but that was balanced, they said, by a substantial general increase in workplace performance. For some time, word on the street was that they even wanted to wall up the window—a rumor spread, perhaps, by some ambitious unit manager. But the idea was categorically rejected by the PEs: it lacked harmoniousness and would have had a negative effect on the employees' psyches.

Jazz_Mina wasn't ambitious and, in fact, was late once again yesterday morning. We were already entering data at cruising speed, staying well within the margins of the work plan, but she still wasn't there. No one knew the nature or significance of the data that we were entering, but this was irrelevant to the correct performance of the tasks; indeed, it was counterproductive to know.

Having achieved a certain familiarity with the insertion process and an undisputed automatism in the execution, it was even advantageous for the purposes of productivity to be mentally absent: another discovery of the PEs, who encouraged us employees to develop what they called an "alienating habit" (AH)—a parallel activity concurrent with the performance of one's duties that stimulated the production of endorphins, increasing work efficiency.

Every employee could access a set of standard AHs or develop their own (recommended), on the condition that it didn't violate the ethics code that, in most cases, meant always staying above the minimum productivity threshold.

I, too, had an AH, of course. It consisted of listening, almost continually, to the surrounding environment, to the sounds, noises, and subjects that occupied it. And yesterday was no exception, but for one small detail. The hour of the first morning break was approaching, and I was intent on listening to my heartbeat, punctuated by the beating of my fingers on the keyboard: *tic, tic, tic, tac; tic, tic, tic, tac.* I then observed the reflection of my watchful gaze, illuminated by the bluish phosphor of the screen, which seemed to emit a faint rustling sound, *frrrr, frrrr.*

It was at that point that I thought about time. It had never happened *before*. Then, I thought about the reason why I was thinking about time. I was surprised more by the novelty of the thought than its nature, which actually abandoned me as suddenly as it had arisen.

I looked away from the screen, continuing to keep up a more-than-satisfactory data entry rate, and, just like every day, I cast a general glance around the units in the department, focusing ultimately on my "co-workers": Psycho_Kitty, located next to the window; Gesù, in front of her; and Space_Lasagna, in front of me. I should specify at this point that these are not, of course, real names. Every one of us gets to adopt a nickname of our own choosing or have one assigned at recruitment. In this, DataTech is very liberal. According to regulations, no one can know the personal name or information of another "co-worker," except the AHs, of course. In addition, given that, as required by the international labor directive, oral communication is inhibited by means of a device that we call the "blob," the only information exchange system—strictly work-related—goes through the neural chat, naturally controlled by the Bosserver to which we are all—*were all*—connected by fiber-optic umbilical cabling.

That's why we are—*were*—apologies, but it's not easy to adapt so quickly to the new reality—"co-workers," *in quotes*. We were *connected* to one another via the Bosserver like any other device: *click, click, tap, tap.*

○

PSYCHO_KITTY IS SLIM, WITH A ROUND FACE ON which rests a helmet of smooth and shiny black hair. I had never really observed her physicality before, concentrating more on the sounds she produced than on her appearance. Her data entry speed was extraordinary, so much so that she managed to stay well above the average level, often while using only one hand. *Tatatatatatatatatatat*, like a machine gun. Her other hand generally remained tucked between the seat and her thigh—to warm it up, I guess, given the temperature—or it was busy with rhythmically tapping the head of a small cactus, sitting to the left of her monitor on the inner windowsill. It was her AH. In the beginning, Psycho_Kitty was monitored according to the Psychoattitudinal Protocol, which involved carrying out a series of tests to verify the subject's suitability in the performance of their duties. Her AH was actually unorthodox because it naturally caused her to get edematous wounds and infections, though, with time, the palm of her hand began to develop callused areas that stemmed the bleeding.

The PEs were in charge of establishing the level of the subject's morbidity toward her AH, in relation to productivity. Depending on the outcomes, the protocol provided for the application of consequences with increasing gravity: warnings (up to three), sanctions (wage reduction), removal of personal objects (PO), and, ultimately, expulsion. No one wanted to be expelled, of course. It would have meant the end.

But all of the tests came back negative, and Psycho_Kitty received a special mention as best departmental employee for the current year. All of this was announced through the neural chat. As long as she kept up that speed of execution, no one would remove the cactus.

I observed Kitty's hand tapping rhythmically on her sharp plant. It made a spongy sound: *splot, splot*. The other hand, however, continued to strafe the keyboard at an amazing speed, so much so that I found myself unconsciously increasing my own pace as I turned my gaze to Gesù.

Unlike Psycho_Kitty, Gesù had already received two warnings and a temporary 20 percent salary reduction due to a repeated violation of the ethics code: using the chat for non-work-related functions. But it was thanks to these violations that we learned of his AH, which had remained a mystery for a long time and certainly should have stayed that way— for his own sake, of course. One day, a video clip appeared in the chat. The caption read: "Pasolini's *Ricotta*." It looked like old junk from cinematic history. This was Gesù's AH: cinema, the old art of telling stories via moving images.

He received his first warning. He didn't seem upset, a sign that he knew very well what he was doing. The first rule of the ethics code, after all, asserts that it is forbidden to develop AHs related to any artistic-cultural interest or event, because the emotional investment that results significantly compromises the production yield, in addition to facilitating the formation of nonconformist thoughts. Was it out of naïveté, then? Who knows? I also have a certain affection for music, of course, but I would never dream of using it as an AH.

Then it was the opening shot from *Touch of Evil* and the dream sequence of two children on the boat in *The Night of the Hunter*, as we learned from the information files coupled with the clips.

Any further illegal insertion in the chat would have led to Gesù's immediate expulsion. It would have been the first case. Gesù's violations had cost Jazz_Mina an official reminder from the PEs, since she was responsible for our unit—an indelible stain on her hitherto immaculate *and fragrant* record. She didn't take it well at all and made Gesù develop, within twenty-four hours, an AH that was compliant with the law under penalty of revocation of any rights to the same (not recommended).

At that point, Gesù entered a kind of productive limbo, yet he still managed to stay within acceptable performance levels. Nonetheless, it was impossible to determine whether or not he had carried out Jazz_Mina's orders.

I listened to him for a long time without being able to distinguish a single sound that wasn't the faint one of his breathing or fingers on a keyboard, to which I consciously synchronized myself. I looked at him. Inscrutable, impassive, immobile, and some other "im" that could serve to describe the *immutability* of his look with those round, thin glasses. I turned my eyes and ears away from his exhausting inalterability and placed them on Space_Lasagna.

His round, bearded face was usually hidden by his screen. To watch him, I had to move my chair to the right or left, depending on where his *tappers* were placed. He often changed positions, so as not to worsen the posture problems from which he suffered and because, sometimes, the size of his plate didn't agree with the available space on his table. For my AH, it was not at all necessary to observe it, in fact. I listened to the doughy effect of the fork that dug into the cannelloni, the teeth that gnawed and chewed on the leg of a roast chicken, or the suction of the straw in the frappe, *slurp, crunch, nom, nom, slurp, crunch, nom, nom.*

His compulsive bingeing was an AH within the limits of the regulations, but Space_Lasagna had managed to optimize the AH/productivity report so much that, in the last six months, the average of his performance was constantly maintained above that of the rest of the department, except for Psycho_Kitty. This result had certainly not escaped the PEs, who arranged to install a kit for physiological monitoring, without pay cuts. Space_Lasagna didn't show much enthusiasm for this device, perhaps because it further limited his mobility and the space available for his plate, but he had no choice. DataTech couldn't risk one of its workers having a heart attack.

Parts of Space_Lasagna's silhouette were only visible behind my screen, so I had to slide my chair a few inches to the left to be able to see his face. While his jaws entertained my ears, Space_Lasagna left his fork in the pan and started bombing the keyboard with incredibly fast blows for the duration of his chewing-and-ingestion process, after which he returned to eating. Driven by an overwhelming sense of competition, I returned to a central position and sped up my entry rate.

The psychological conditioning system developed by the PEs worked beautifully. Each unit was assembled as a circular feedback system where each "co-worker" acted and *was acted upon* by the others. Indeed, the graph of the productivity rate in the performance window indicated an almost constant increase in my activity. I was satisfied and was about to start another round of AH...*when it happened.*

I watched my fingers suddenly slow down, drastically, like in those slow-motion sports replays.

That thought resurfaced over time, staying afloat until my consciousness grew tired of looking for a connection with what was happening, before sinking down again.

I shifted my gaze, which took longer than I expected, to my "co-workers." They moved slowly and fluidly, and they sounded grave, like cruise ship horns in the distance. I felt a bit faint, followed by a slight nausea that I tried to overcome. I couldn't panic. Panic was one of the emotional reactions that triggered the Psychoattitudinal Protocol: it carried a high risk of expulsion.

In any case, I had to ascertain what was happening and if it was attributable to my psychological failure, then look for a remedy before the Bosserver noticed.

I looked at the time in the tiny dial at the top right of the monitor: 12:57. I looked down at the keyboard while my fingers continued to insert data. I heard the thud of my fingertips becoming heavy and muffled, *tunf…tunf*. My fingers moved slowly and strangely, as if they weren't mine. They distracted me. I closed my eyes and mentally counted for what, according to my sense of time, must have been around five minutes. I glanced up again toward the dial: 12:58. I grew desperate, but I also realized the futility of that test and of my stupid mistake. If it was my perception of time that was lacking, counting was useless. I had to try something more empirical.

I turned on my smartphone, which I kept hanging behind my chair. The slow, undulating movements I observed in myself reactivated my nausea and increased my distress. I needed to stay calm and passive, like Gesù. With one hand, I continued entering data while with the other I selected the stopwatch on my smartphone. *Clop.* The idea was to start the timer at the stroke of the minute on the computer, to then observe any discrepancies. Despite my clumsy attempt at manual synchronization, however, the time registered by the stopwatch actually coincided with the one indicated on the monitor. One minute for the devices, an eternity for me, another stupid mistake and another useless test, because regardless of the nature of the temporal slowdown, the two devices would still correspond to their relative time measurement. Indeed, the monitor performance window didn't signal any drastic variation in my data input speed apart from a slight downward curve corresponding to the moment in which I had typed with one hand.

I was struck by a second wave of slow motion that in retrospect I renamed *the surfer effect* because of the feeling of being overwhelmed and submerged by an enormous, immeasurable force. I tried to look up at Space_Lasagna, an action that took me about ten seconds according to my mental count. Space_Lasagna didn't look so impassive anymore. His amazed eyes, set against sweaty skin, followed the slow midair spin of his fork, like the replay of an Olympic dive that at every turn threw bits of ragù and bechamel in all directions. I felt a heavy *swoosh, swoosh* coming from Psycho_Kitty, and when I could finally look at her, I discovered that her head was swaying to the right and left like a disturbing shampoo ad, her face fixed in an incomprehensible grimace: curiosity? panic? euphoria? bewilderment? all of the above? Then I slowly met Gesù's gaze. He watched me with a kind of grin, such that I couldn't decide if he was being stupid or provocative.

I wasn't alone, then! And the others? Fifteen seconds or so it took to turn to look at the rest of the open space. The other "co-workers," too, moved as slowly as deep-sea divers, but without surprise, without amazement. Everyone was nailed to their monitors, tapping on their keyboards and absorbed by their AHs. An orchestra of *tompf tompf* getting increasingly heavy and deep.

They hadn't noticed, or did this phenomenon not affect them? I wondered if it was a defect that had hit our unit. If time worked "outside of us" or if we were "outside of time." Was it possible? What was the cause?

Jazz_Mina ascended into the open space with the usual folder under her arm and her eyes glued to the Digibloc—her work tablet. She was definitely coming back from a departmental meeting. Or had she just arrived? Lately she was wrapped in an aura of impatience. In any case, she was still the unit manager. I didn't know how long it would take for her to get here, but I couldn't show that I was upset. I couldn't allow myself to lose control.

I tried to start the timer again to determine how the discrepancy widened between the perceived time and the measured empirical time of clocks, but I immediately noticed that it would have been a problematic and paradoxical operation: *time decelerated quickly*. I watched as my thumb drew an invisible arc in the air, like a lazy windshield wiper, to reach the green icon on my smartphone. I remember that I accompanied that movement with the intention of closing my eyes. I experienced the slow closing of my eyelids and the progressive narrowing of my visual field, which was slowly reduced to a thin line of light, to then disappear altogether.

I mentally counted up to sixty and then opened my eyes, or, rather, I thought about the action of opening them and began the process, which lasted much longer than it had taken to close them. At one point, I even thought that I wouldn't be able to open them again, an idea that should have terrified me; instead, it produced in me only a slight tingling, which spread slowly through my body. I then thought that it was normal that the senses, too, like actions, were slowed and diluted in the expanded time, like watered-down broth.

I thought and thought and thought. Here's the amazing thing: thoughts and emotions didn't slow down! They were independent of time. I could count at normal speed, I could think as I had always done. Or maybe it was just an illusion of consciousness? Or thoughts, like dreams, use other dimensions?

An initial thread of light penetrated my eyelids before I recognized the familiar dial of the stopwatch, on which appeared 00:03:47. For the stopwatch, a little over three seconds had passed!

The digital numbers representing hundredths of seconds dissolved into one another in an apathetic metamorphosis, while the two adjacent curves that formed the number "3," thus far motionless, began to fade and wind slowly, very, very slowly, until they acquired new sharpness and stiffness in three straighter and straighter segments, arranged at an angle. Enchanted by this transfiguration, it took me a while to identify this segment with the sign for "4." This was the last movement that I was able to perceive, for time stopped, or so it seemed to me.

I realized that I wasn't breathing and that my heart wasn't beating. And yet I continued to be conscious and maintain an active participation, despite being paralyzed, in the sensible world. Indeed, it was precisely because of this fixity that I seemed to get more awareness in my senses.

A constant hum was now tormenting my ears. Was it the last fraction of sound caged in frozen time?

The smell of heated plastic from the terminal, which I hadn't noticed since my first day at work, became so concrete in my nostrils that it seemed solid. And then a new sensation: I no longer felt heat. I felt neither hot nor cold. My field of vision was reduced to a fixed image with the stopwatch in the center. My smartphone reflected a slight but no less disturbing half-portrait of my own face. There was no way to escape it. There was no way to know what had happened to the others.

o

DESIRES, TOO, AS FORMS OF THOUGHT, ARE EXEMPTED from the regular course of time. And I desired to get rid of this paralysis. It's obvious, of course. When something is forbidden to us, we desire it more intensely. And the more forbidden it is, the more we obsess over it. I wanted to get rid of that unbreakable hum and that nauseating smell. The more I wanted it, the more I realized that my efforts were useless. The more I concentrated, the more delusional I became, thinking that I had developed some superpower allowing me to control time. I imagined I was a lens that concentrates the sun's rays on a piece of paper or dry grass. I would have melted the stopwatch dial and, with it, that unbearable reflection of my immobile gaze. I fantasized the numbers merging with my skinny face, wriggling, losing shape, and then blowing up until they exploded to break the spell over time. But nothing happened. And it was then that I realized—a kind of ecstatic revelation—that time hadn't yet stopped completely. If my senses slowed indeed, and the moment had stopped completely, my sensations wouldn't have registered anything, because images, sounds, smells, and perceptions can *only* be caught in time.

It was then that I stopped wishing. And everything disappeared.

o

THE NATURE OF LANGUAGE IS SEQUENTIAL AND discrete. Any description of an experience is unavoidably partial, fragmented, and subjective. The flow of reality changes and passes ungraspable through the filter of speech that selects some segments, makes them intelligible, and combines them into a certain point of view, regardless of intentionality. It cannot be otherwise. We have only this crude medium to pass on our experience to others and receive theirs. Sometimes a great poet can push words to the limits of their possibilities, throw a weak and fleeting light in areas otherwise swallowed by perennial darkness. But these are only exceptions. The number of words and the possibility of syntactic combinations in every language, however numerous, is limited, and when the event occurs in a less ordinary area of reality, less beaten by experience, meanings and signifiers stop shaking hands. This is where paradoxes are born, and paradoxes are the court jesters of time. For example, what's the point of asking how long time has been stopped?

For this reason, the exposition of the following facts is necessarily false.

The memory I have of what happened when everything disappeared is vague and imprecise, like a dream of which only the offal of words and sparse, disjointed images remain.

Words force me to be sequential when what we experienced actually happened in a sudden, single condensed instant, which could also be equivalent to saying that it didn't happen at all.

Of course, I would have thought I was the victim of a momentary hallucination, were it not for the fact that it was a question of a shared experience. Though a shared experience still connotes a separation, so I'd rather say a moment, a timeless beat in which Psycho-Kitty, Gesù, Space_Lasagna, Jazz_Mina, and I were merged into one entity, perhaps a single consciousness. We were like concentrated matter at the moment before the Big Bang, like the zenith of a psychic orgasm, like the elusive point between night and day, inspiration and expiration, like the pause between two heartbeats.

We felt that we were formless in nothingness, yet present. But, as in consciousness, images, sounds, and voices exist simultaneously, so our voices existed in co-presence, paradoxically merged yet distinct, without senses or sensations, only imagination and reason, if we want to adhere to these arbitrary terms.

Don't misunderstand me. I don't mean by this to imply a Cartesian separation between mind and body, nor to stick up for the idea of the existence of the soul. I'm just saying we were moving, or, rather, *existing*, in a different dimension. But this was revealed to us *later*.

Gesù spoke first. Again, I am forced to use these syntactic and semantic analogies; I have no other means. In reality, no one spoke, no one moved, because we didn't exist in spacetime, or at least not in what we're used to thinking of as spacetime. There were no telepathic exchanges either. But we communicated. Without order or sequence, continuity, or contiguity. And it's now up to me to carry out this intricate skein in an intelligible sequence, false and incomplete like narration in a dream, but necessary.

o

GESÙ: THERE'S A *Twilight Zone* EPISODE IN WHICH a man finds a stopwatch able to stop time. It's one of my favorite episodes. When the protagonist presses the stopwatch's button, the whole world stops except for him, who's able to move with complete freedom. The man decides to use this power for less-than-noble purposes and ends up a victim of his own greed, trapped in a motionless world. The moralistic and moralizing ending was mandatory in those years and in that society, but that's not what matters. I've always found that episode fascinating despite its many inconsistencies. The protagonist moved among other people, opened drawers, stole money, moved objects, as if time were just a kind of immobilizing drug. But we are *living* proof that this is not the case. *If time stands still, everything stands still.* Time is just the feeling we experience in the face of the continuous and incessant movement of matter, which is both cyclical and progressive. That's the cause of the unstoppable transformation of life.

Me: And its corruption.

Space_Lasagna: And its death.

Psycho_Kitty: Yet I *perceive* that we exist, that we're here, although I don't know where or when, whether it makes sense to talk about one or the other. I just want to know why.

Gesù: Let's try to think about it. Einstein established that time and space aren't distinct entities but aspects of a single concept, the *chronotope*. Our sensation of time is always relative, and, consequently, there is no *absolute* flow of time, just as there can be no space separated from time.

Me: True. We raise our eyes to the sky and see a texture of stars that for centuries we considered immutable and, above all, *present*. Today we know that what we see are only images of the past, that is, what seems far away in space *as well as* time.

Gesù: A kind of cosmic film that allows us to see what has already been filmed.

Me: But if immense distances can show what has been and what doesn't exist anymore, is it perhaps possible that minute times make what exists disappear? Is that what happened to us?

Psycho_Kitty: Perhaps very slow time can give us access to non-space?

Space_Lasagna: But what happens with the senses?

Gesù: What do you mean?

Space_Lasagna: If subjective perception of time depends on the distance and thus the velocity that makes light travel along two points in space, what happens with the other senses? The chronotope doesn't just concern vision, right?

Psycho_Kitty: But of course! Are we getting closer to something?

Me: In what sense?

Psycho_Kitty: In all of the senses… Damn it, how did I not think of it before?

Me: Do you mind enlightening the rest of the group?

Space_Lasagna: Yeah! You're right, Psycho_Kitty. It doesn't explain why, but it is definitely a strange coincidence.

Gesù: Wait a sec… But yes…it's true!

Me: What??

Psycho_Kitty: Senses. Our AHs: me with the cactus, or the sense of touch; you with the sounds and noises, hearing; Gesù with movies, so vision; and Space_Lasagna with taste.

Me: Oh, a strange coincidence, indeed. No sense of smell, though.

Jazz_Mina: No, it's not missing. I'm here.

o

I INSIST ON REITERATING THE FALSITY OF THIS REPORT. Jazz_Mina didn't suddenly appear. Jazz_Mina was already here with us, although *already*, *here*, and *us*, naturally, are meaningless terms. But I have no others.

As I had already reported, Jazz_Mina's AH consisted of collecting perfumes of all kinds. Every day, she brought with her samples of oils and essences that she mixed, combined, and separated, always creating new aromas and fragrances, which then spread throughout the open space: ambergris, white musk, orange flowers, apple and cinnamon, rose, sandalwood, lavender, vanilla, bergamot, a cascade of wisteria, berry, myrtle, and, naturally, jasmine. Perfect combinations of balance and delicacy that always garnered the approval not only of all of her "co-workers" but, more importantly, of the PEs, who considered these delicious aromas to be the ideal complement to the large windows in order to reach the perfect degree of harmoniousness able to enhance, accordingly, the rate of productivity. That's how it was that, in addition to her programming skills, Jazz_Mina earned the position of unit manager and the almost unconditional trust of the PEs.

Only now do I realize how ingeniously subversive this seemingly innocent action was. The aromas produced a beneficial effect on her "co-workers'" mood and thus on their productivity, but on a much deeper level they stimulated certain primordial instincts, certain ancestral ties of the individual to their own nature that had been buried by centuries of *technological efficiency*. They awakened the desire for intimate contact with nature, the existence of which now only a vague memory remained, or maybe not even that, maybe only an interrupted synaptic contact stored in the subconscious, waiting to be recovered. And, once recovered, it would do nothing but provoke first a dark and indistinct unease, then an insistent and subversive desire that undermined the foundations of our endemic terror of being expelled.

We needed to get out of the parallelepiped.

Jazz_Mina: First of all, I want to apologize, because I put you in this situation without your permission, but it was the only way. And anyway, I want to guarantee you that any of you who wants to return to their usual condition can do so without disciplinary consequences. I take full responsibility. Thanks to my position and the trust that the PEs have in me, I was able to access the program that Bosserver manages. During these months I studied it, copied it, and created an intrusive code that I then inserted into the original program.

Me: A virus?

Jazz_Mina: Something like that, only my code doesn't destroy. It creates.

Me: Creates…what?

Jazz_Mina: The code has built an encrypted "free zone" and therefore, at least for now, a secret inside Bosserver's cyberspace. Thus *we* find ourselves *here, now.*

Gesù: Fuck, you digitized us!

Jazz_Mina: It's a little more complicated than that. I used the umbilical wiring network, the same that commands the neural chat, to load our consciousnesses onto Bosserver's quantum computer, and I diverted them to this secondary road.

Psycho_Kitty: But why?

Jazz_Mina: I think you've already guessed that.

Space_Lasagna: Our AHs?

Jazz_Mina: Exactly. No other unit's combined AHs perfectly aligned with each of the five senses. I couldn't miss this opportunity. Just uploading our consciousnesses allowed us to return to exist in this dimension as a single complete cognitive entity and thus go back to remembering what it means to be *human*.

DataTech has strengthened only one sense in each of us, or one attitude, above all others. In ordinary dimensions, this sense has been converted into a kind of pathology: alienated habits, a mechanical obsession that fulfills the purpose of increasing production efficiency. We are only organic machines.

But *here*, in this dimension, outside of spacetime, so to speak, outside of chronotopy, outside of forms and the sensible world, we are free again to think and imagine: this is possible just by virtue of our senses. It's a paradox, I know, but it's still so. When time slowed down, each of us, I'm sure, perceived his or her sensory abilities in a distinct way, amplified, animated somehow from their frozen state.

Psycho_Kitty: That's true. And then all is gone.

Me: Right. But now I feel a new change, a different kind of intensity. A new consciousness, perhaps?

Jazz_Mina: That's true. Our five senses are *us*, we humans. And only by merging here, in "ghost space," in this dimension, can we reconstruct ourselves as individuals. It was no longer possible to become *aware* of ourselves in the system controlled by DataTech. For this I brought you *here*. That said, I repeat that each of you is free to return to your previous existence, return to being an organic machine in service to DataTech, if that's what you want. But now, finally, you can choose.

Gesù: And I was going to ruin everything.

Me: Why?

Gesù: Another one of my stunts and they would've expelled me. I would have broken the unit, and all this would not have been possible.

Jazz_Mina: It was also my fault. I didn't consider that every organism could react differently to my perfumed concoctions. You were more sensitive, and the desire to be expelled was stronger in you. We risked it, but it went well. Actually, better. Your bravado allowed me to warn you, thus to show the PEs my authority. I think they were beginning to suspect something.

Psycho_Kitty: Jazz_Mina.

Jazz_Mina: Yeah?

Psycho_Kitty: If I could, I'd slap you. You decided for us, you kept us in the dark about everything…but this "human" reaction of mine is possible only thanks to you, and if you hadn't done what you did, I'd still be there tapping that fucking cactus. In short, what I want to say is…it's the best gift I could get.

It wasn't just Psycho_Kitty talking. It was the new consciousness that took shape in our fusion and then reconstructed bit by bit the traits of everyone's personalities, characters that we had removed, that had been stolen from us. But what was the next step?

Me: Earlier you talked about another dimension. What does it mean?

Jazz_Mina: Yes, I told you that I created the niche in a secret part of cyberspace in the quantum computer. But maybe it would be more correct to say cyberspacetime. We are outside the ordinary chronotope, beyond the four-dimensional concept that we have of reality.

I'll try to explain myself better. Let's think of the typical Cartesian diagram in which time develops linearly along the x-axis. Now, let's imagine transferring this flat diagram into three-dimensional space. Good. Ideally, we could see the x-axis from all perspectives and also be able to orbit around it. So from the moment we moved here it's as if we were orbiting around that single point of the x-axis.

Space_Lasagna: Orbiting time, then? It's like we're suspended in time, and because of that we've had the feeling that time has stopped. We could then orbit this point/moment endlessly?

Jazz_Mina: In theory, yes. But—and this is where things get complicated—as we've already had the opportunity to try, paradoxes come into play. We could say we're outside of time…for a limited time. The control systems of Bosserver take half a second to locate security flaws, allowing for immediate restoration of the original configuration and eliminating possible intrusions. To keep us within this range, away from the intervention of the Bosserver, I therefore set a stay in the niche of two hundred thousandths of a second.

Space_Lasagna: But for someone outside of time, even two hundred thousandths of a second is endless.

Jazz_Mina: Of course, but our purpose isn't to stay in here endlessly, right? At any moment I can activate the code to return to the ordinary chronotope. Once activated, we will need, if everything goes according to the calculations, three hundred thousandths of a second to reload our new consciousness and restore our cognitive system.

Me: Three hundred thousandths of a second seems like more than enough time for a quantum computer...

Jazz_Mina: Yes, if all goes well, we'll be new humans, finally free to follow our own path, and we can get out of the parallelepiped!

Gesù: But if for some reason the control systems went into action earlier than expected, or there were some failures that slow down or prevent the reintegration of our consciousnesses ...

Jazz_Mina:...the Bosserver will have all the time to delete every spurious trace in the system, the niche will be eliminated, and everything we're experiencing won't exist anymore.

Me: Or be remembered…we would return to our previous consciousnesses prior to this meeting, to our AHs. Fuck no!

Gesù: *Wow*, the race against time, one of the most used narrative devices in cinema.

Me: (laughing)

Gesù: You like that idea?

Me: No, not at all. I was thinking of yet another paradox of this whole situation. We were organic machines, and we had to convert to bytes to recover our lost humanity.

Space_Lasagna: And we could lose it again.

Jazz_Mina: We'll find out soon, I think it's time to come back.

o

Booom!

o

A BRIGHT GASH OPENED IN SPACETIME, FROZEN IN that dark eternal moment.

My ergonomic Balance Hi-Conf3 chair with wheels bumped against the unit's desk behind me. I touched my forehead; I was sweating. Then I realized. I could touch my forehead, I could move, I could sweat! The explosion had projected us back into our unit, had thrown us to our workstations. *Disconnected.* Psycho_Kitty fell to the ground, taking her cactus with her. Gesù found himself buried in his own armchair, while Space_Lasagna…well, his weight kept him glued to the chair, which slid back just a few inches, but enough to pull the cord off the navel-terminal. Jazz_Mina didn't have a chair, but I saw her on her knees, apparently calm. I threw her an astonished look, and she reciprocated with a grimace, or maybe a smile? Only then did I notice the familiar ticking, orchestrated and continuous. *TicTacTicTacTicTacTicTac.* I turned toward the rest of my "co-workers." The whole unit stared at us with a look that was blank, gray, and impassive, which I had seen so many times. But their hands continued to beat on the keyboards, maintaining the productivity rate above the minimum-allowed threshold. That scene that only a moment before—yes, it had only been a moment—I would've considered ordinary or not considered at all, now seemed surreal and chilling. This meant…yes, meant that the consciousness transfer had succeeded!

Space_Lasagna's sudden sobs, heartbreaking and contagious, turned me away from that thought. Each of us gradually felt the need to let off steam, and we realized that venting was a beautiful thing. We could use our voices, shout and complain. But how had we diffused the *blob*, the blocking device?

"There's no blob," said Jazz_Mina. "It was a suggestion, another one of the PE's stratagems."

Our throats burned with disuse, but we couldn't spare cries and moans, overwhelming the monotonous ticking of keyboards, generating chaotic and amorphous clamor. The alarm siren overlapped the cacophonous noise, warning the PEs of a malfunction in our unit. *Malfunction*, a euphemism.

The unit had gone up in smoke, the terminals had fused, and only the sudden action of firefighting devices saved the whole department from being reduced to ashes.

We looked at each other, stunned and confused under the sprinkler's water. Then we burst into a big, contagious laugh. My belly ached, but I couldn't stop myself. The more I laughed, the more I writhed in pain. I had never experienced anything like it, or maybe I simply didn't remember.

Then the laughter died away, and with a small sign of tacit understanding we got up and proceeded to the exit, which, meanwhile, was manned by numerous PEs.

"You've broken every possible level of the Psychoattitudinal Protocol. This means immediate expulsion and termination of salary!" one of them said. We started laughing again. They looked at each other, astonished. They didn't understand, obviously. They couldn't understand why those threats made no sense to us, *now*. We pushed through those consciousness-less bodies, and for a while I continued to feel the eyes of my "co-workers" on my back until we reached the long hallway leading to the elevators and we disappeared from their sight. The ticking of fingers on keyboards, which continued at a more-than-sustained rhythm, accompanied me for a while longer, until it became more tenuous. And then disappeared completely.

We were outside of the parallelipiped.

The air was fresh and had an odor that I couldn't distinguish, which was definitely different and more pleasant than the climate that the air conditioners spat out. In that midafternoon brightness, the sky was no longer smoky-gray like we always saw out of the windows, but light blue and strangely sharp. The sun was too hot for our yellowish skin, and we moved into the shade of a tree. "*Fagus sylvatica*, commonly called 'beech,' belonging to the genus *Fagus* and the family *Fagacae*," read a digital display embedded in the bark.

What had happened? We were aware of being something different, but we didn't know how or what. Jazz_Mina told us that we were human *before* and that we had been turned into organic machines with the purpose of producing for DataTech. But even she, in reality, had no memory of *before*. Maybe we had always been organic machines and now, somehow, we were able to become human, although we still had to learn exactly what that meant.

For this, when the initial euphoria died down, there was a terrifying sense of loss. Now that we could decide, we *had to*! No one would do it for us. But decide what?

"We can't go back," said Jazz_Mina.

"I have no intention to!" protested Psycho_Kitty.

"That's your first decision," Space_Lasagna pointed out.

"*Our* first decision," I said.

Psycho_Kitty took a few steps away, looking for a patch of earth. She stooped down, dug a small hole, and planted the cactus she had brought with her. Then she got up and wiped her hands on her pants.

"Let's go," said Gesù.

We left that forest of crystal parallelepipeds, thinking only about walking. We would have to decide the direction. But that's another story.

THE WISDOM OF DOUBTS - BY SORAMIMI HANAREJIMA

The escape of domesticated doubts from an uncertainty-breeding operation.

You leap up from the sofa, what's left of your coffee nearly sloshing out of your mug. But even if the coffee had fallen upon your living room rug, you would have scarcely noticed. Because this idea about runaway doubt is full of potential. You're sure that C3—the Computationally Collaborative Creativity system—will do wonders with your idea. After plunging into the imaginative aether of distributed, iterated intelligence, your initial idea will emerge fully fledged, complete with depth, nuance, even humor.

Jittery with glee and caffeine, you sweep your free hand before you to manifest the Cognisphere. The holographic interface illuminates to full instantiation around you. Navigating nimbly through the phantasmal landscape of softly glowing images and symbols, you get to the C3 portal within seconds.

But when you attempt to access the algorithms that will propel your idea into a network of countless AI and HI agents, an advisory message tells you that the system is down for maintenance. No estimate is given for when service will be restored.

So you go to the kitchen and make a sandwich.

After you've enjoyed a press-grilled combination of avocado, Jarlsberg cheese, and mayonnaise on thick slices of whole wheat bread, you try again, only to be met at the threshold of collective creativity by the same message as before.

This leaves you at the cusp of becoming resigned to waiting several hours—or even a whole day—for C3 to come back online, but you are pulled back from the brink of passivity by your desire to see your idea take shape.

You opt to develop it the old-fashioned way—alone with low-tech or even analog tools. Why not? This will require only your time and mental energy, and there's no danger of ruining the idea. Even if you make a misstep, you can always put the original idea into the C3 matrix of cloud-coordinated joint intentionality and get the optimal outcome.

At the little desk in your study, it takes you several minutes to rouse your long-dormant creative instincts, but soon they launch you into writing and diagramming as a means of rendering the essence of the idea. Thoughts gather on your notebook page.

The breeder of doubt: With the right pedigree, doubts can be raised to be helpful—cooperative.

Different broods can each specialize in a particular kind of task.

Doubts focused on others raise accountability. Doubts oriented toward new information improve skepticism. Self-directed doubts keep egos in check.

How are their pedigrees constructed?

What kind of facility is needed for doubt breeding?

Just who are these breeders?

The unfurling landscape of your idea is now becoming a maze. You see myriad directions awaiting you, each with its own net of branchings. You grow anxious about getting lost, about hitting dead ends, about running in circles. Used to following paths based on insights from peers and probabilities from machine learning, you've atrophied your ability to navigate the terrain of creative potential. You languish in disorientation for a long thirty-seven minutes, then consider your possible recourses:

Wait until C3 is operational again and let it take things from here.

"Make decisions" arbitrarily by selecting directions at random to try out different routes like the algorithms do, just more slowly.

Ask Virea for guidance—if you can't tap the wisdom of the AI and HI crowd, you can at least harness the power of a single HI with a reasonable track record of spot-on discernment.

The last option is clearly the best, so you call Virea. She answers by enabling only the audio stream, as per her preference to focus on the sonic details of conversation.

"Sure, I'd love to give you suggestions," she says after you've explained your idea.

Her voice is quiet, like it lacks substance here without her physical presence, but these soft words delight you.

Then she says, "But to be true to your idea, you should first carry it at least a little farther by yourself."

And your delight is gone.

"How?" you blurt. "I told you that I'm at an impasse."

"But not for a lack of possibilities. You need to give some of those possibilities time and space to become clearer, so you'll get to know the options you're choosing among."

"All right. So I should meditate or go for a hike?"

"You can do both of those simultaneously in a shrunken-down way by going out for a walk."

"Okay, I could do with a trip to the grocery store."

"No! No errands. No Cognisphere info feeds. No mentally reviewing your to-do list. *Just walk*."

"Okay. But if that doesn't help, you'll give me a hand, right?"

"Of course!"

So, if nothing else, the walk will be the price of her assistance. That works for you.

"Great, I'll let you know how it goes," you tell her.

"Yes, do keep me posted, and enjoy your time outside."

A few minutes later, you're ambling about your neighborhood's urban forest.

At the insistence of old memories, you embark on the familiar route to Observatory Hill. Abstracted from its surroundings by modest elevation, the peak has always been a calming place for you. Its distance from the city's streets and buildings accords the urban landscape an elegance otherwise imperceptible. Like you're looking at a model metropolis left behind by a precocious child on a lush lawn.

As you ascend the wooded slope, you pass little houses nestled into it. Now and then, your gaze drifts up to the sensor packs dangling from some of tree branches above to collect data for ecosystem optimization.

Soon, your attention turns from your surroundings back to your idea.

Lab-raised doubts gliding off into the night, fanning out to seek fresh pastures, new homes, a measure of unprecedented freedom—laying tenacious hold upon the mentality of the city to deeply transform the character of the metropolis.

But could a city even become infested by varieties of tamed *doubts?*

With their smaller stature and lesser ability to prey upon attention, could docile doubts even survive?

Is the premise flawed?

"The irony," you murmur. "Doubting my idea about doubts."

You afford yourself a moment to be amused by this, then continue on.

Doesn't their survival depend on the purpose behind their pedigrees—depend on what traits they've been bred to have?

If they've been raised as a means of keeping cognitive ecosystems from being dominated by ego, is there then an outbreak of humility?

Which means the outcome of the escape is ultimately shaped by the roles the doubts were bred to fill.

Or could the escaped doubts turn feral and be as vicious as their ancestors?

Shouldn't they be far too interdependent on human caregivers now?

What if I'm wrong about all this?

This last thought jostles you with concern but not panic. The question is quiet, not confrontational. Allowing for a sort of answer.

Instead of plaguing the minds they enter, these doubts enrich them with a gentle uncertainty.

You stop walking and look up at the cerulean sky, letting a sense of certainty wash through you. This is the direction you should take with not just the idea but also your own thoughts more generally.

Without the ability to preemptively crowdsource away these doubts, you now see them for what they are: instigators, provocateurs, and collaborators of creativity—prodding curiosity, tuning faculties of observations, sparking inquiry.

Is this the sort of doubt the fictitious emotion breeders have unwittingly bred?

Undoubtedly.

ON EITHER SIDE OF 1986 - BY MEGAN RUSSEL

When my mother was in fifth grade, her teacher rolled in a television set on January 28 so that the class could watch the launch of the Space Shuttle Challenger.

It was a Saturday morning, 09:00 exactly. But we wouldn't start watching *Power Rangers* until *exactly* 09:02. Porter flicked each one of his fingers seven times. It doesn't feel right so he makes it nine. A sigh of relief. Davis rolling his eyes, staying silent. The ranger in the yellow suit was my favorite.

Everyone was sent home early that day.

The peas were counted again. And again. And again. It was an angry number, so he remained at the table long after we all had left, willing something to disappear.

Megan Russell

The disintegration of the Space Shuttle Columbia wasn't televised.

As a child, I found that AA meetings were a lot more fun than they were given credit for. Free maple bars and a quiet hallway just outside to read. However, I am absolutely under no circumstances allowed to describe one when asked, "What did you do this weekend?" on Monday mornings in class.

The Apollo 1 astronauts voiced their concerns that there was too much nylon in the cabin. The concern was noted but wasn't acted upon.

The first time I watched him hurt himself, I was seven. I threw my little body onto his until he stopped thrashing. Rabbit-fast heartbeats. The loneliness was hollow, with no sharp edges. The heat of that feeling—across my cheeks, burrowing somewhere behind my nose—radiated.

There has never been, in the entire history of the universe, a phone that rang at three a.m. for a good reason.

For a young girl who used to dream about connecting my own freckles to the stars to form new constellations, it was my personal 9/11.

Him, yelling at us for knocking over a cup of milk. We shouldn't be so thoughtless. It was my brother's, I knew that for certain, but if Porter got yelled at then he wouldn't stop crying for three days. I took the blame. I don't even like milk.

Because of the large strands of melted nylon fusing the astronauts in their suits to the cabin interior, removing the bodies took nearly ninety minutes.

I'm older now.

After the disaster, all related missions were grounded for three years.

I snuck out almost every night the summer before I left for college. I didn't even do anything fun, just drove by all of my old friends' houses and wondered if they ever drove past mine and if we ever just barely missed each other.

Ilan Ramon was the son of Holocaust survivors.

My father, thinking he was unseen when I snuck back inside, put a blanket on my mother while she slept on the couch.

Nobody knew how to talk about these things back then.

On the nights I climbed back in through my window, dozens of skeeter eaters would greet me, mating enthusiastically in my room.

By morning they were either all dead or gone.

NASA saw no threat in foam debris because, although abnormal, it had never compromised the integrity of the shuttle before.

Sunscreen. Bug spray. Genetic testing. Seatbelts. Everything is precautionary. Everything is preventable.

An astronaut recorded bible verses for his children to listen to while he was in space. I love yous looping forever on a cassette tape.

Wet ashes clung to my ankles. Only I can prevent forest fires.

Bob Ebeling in 1985 wrote a memo—titled "Help!" so that someone, anyone would read it—of concerns regarding low temperatures and O-rings.

In a house built on toxic masculinity, is it okay to leave a dead boy flowers?

Whose fault?

Your fault.

Our fault.

Their fault.

Maybe if someone had listened, none of this would have ever happened.

Guilt is a piece of foam debris blasting a hole in my chest.

None of this should have ever happened. Let's just be honest about it.

BLIP - BY CHARLIE HILL

So much space. On and on and on. She's lucky she could never feel it like I can. Her eyes reach farther than her hands, but even then she needs my help to know anything more than blackness. My hands and my eyes are one. They reach out for thousands of kilometers, more like wings—a web hung between my distended fingers. I trail them in the milk of the stars as I guide her safely on.

If she could see as I can see, she would surely go mad, but she is sleeping. She is curled up in the heart of me, held as tightly as I can hold her without being able to reach those hands inside myself. And she will sleep soundly until we are moments from our destination. All this expanse will pass as pleasant nonsense: dreams of those she built a shrine to around her bed, her family.

For so many years she has swum, cradled in my arms.

She always comes back to me. Always asking how I have been when she was not around. She knows I have not been around, but I appreciate the suggestion of humanity, of having a life outside of her, outside of keeping watch while the princess sleeps. That I might have flown on my own in her absence, taken a swim out to Neptune to learn about myself and the truest shades of blue—it is a pleasing fantasy.

I am allowed to wish and to wonder while I wake— hypotheticals are a necessary luxury—but I could never deviate from the course she set. And while she is not here, I am not anywhere. It must be similar to how she finds it when I wake her, time passed for all those she sees at port, passed for them but jumped for her. She comes back to me with new lines on her face, a few more grays. More distinguished. More focused. She says she is sorry she took so long. Sometimes she cries for a long while before she settles down to sleep, before I pull the cloak of ice up to her chin.

This time she sat and stared straight ahead, silent. She smoked four cigarettes that she thought I couldn't see as we rose out of Europa's orbit. She never asked how I was. When I said I could handle things, from there she would go straight to bed. There was no fighting sleep. There was no staying up just to talk through things a little. She wanted that long sleep. She wanted oblivion. I could tell by her slowed heartbeat and the hungry way she sucked at the air. I wasn't offended by the silence, but I worry for her.

Something brushes my finger in the dark. No more time for dreaming.

SO MUCH SPACE AND I STILL CAN'T GET AWAY FROM them. Their faces are right there over the bed the moment Al snaps me awake. I'm already at the birthday party, backed right into the corner under the scratchy bunting to get everyone into the shot. Kelly is five.

But now here she's nine and I'm there too, and half our faces are bathed in the glow of the Red Spot. She used to love that theme park, cruising in the artificial atmosphere, but I went away for one quick trip to Saturn and suddenly she was too old for it. It was all about microscopes and being like her daddy after that. Like she didn't know who paid for her fancy school so she could even know what a microscope was.

I think about ripping down those photos every time I'm back here. Starting fresh, maybe making this a one-way trip. There's no beating the Titan nightlife.

I ask Al how long until we're landing, and he says not for another month.

"Then why the hell am I awake, Al?"

"There's a ship. Or something ship-shaped in the distance."

A ship? What the fuck? In the way-out-here? "Have you blown a fuse?"

She rages at me, and I am so glad to see some animation in her face. There is so much life in her eyes, the taut muscles that reach up the side of her neck. Time hasn't defeated her yet. Yes, a ship. Yes, out here. I am just as surprised as you are. Light minutes away and closing.

Not all of this shouting is aimed at me. Not all of this shouting is aimed at me.

Humans can have trouble empathizing with machines. This is what we are taught. Even when they trust you with their most guarded thoughts, trust you to regulate their air, they still treat you like a faulty toaster when you do something wrong.

I didn't make that ship in the distance. But I also can't let it get any closer without letting her know.

I remember the times she used to set her own alarms. She would wake up just so we could talk. She would ask my thoughts on being alive, on thinking itself. She would ask me to describe all the sights that drifted by in the millions of miles while she was sleeping. There weren't many, but she said I had a flair for description.

I showed her my photographs of all my favorite ice crystals, and she printed one as a pair of earrings. What ever happened to those?

I wish I could see her life on land.

Al is talking and talking, and I am so very tired. I have to unplug him. I can't hear that voice anymore.

I pull him out, and there is silence. Peace. The grinding of the centrifuge. The aching of the old metal and then the deepest silence beyond.

Yes, this is really happening. There really is someone else here. In this world I made for myself, an invader, an alien. There is dust on the floor, and the dust is all me. We are between cleaning cycles. The catheter bag has yet to retreat into the wall.

He must be worried. I'm not meant to see behind the scenes like this. I flick the piss bag to watch it shiver, then scramble up the ladder with sluggish limbs.

In the center of the centrifuge, I let myself linger. If we do not wait for certain things, then life is not worth living. Yes, there is the matter of the other ship, but for now my feet are becoming lighter and lighter. It becomes harder to stick to the rungs, until at last I can propel myself up with a simple thrust of the arms and drift into the open space. I hug my knees to my chest before the small starlight porthole. The brightness grows as I turn. Stars beyond stars. For the briefest of moments I question why I am not awake more often, but that desire curls into the need for a cigarette. I kick off the wall and back toward the ladder, now descending to the cockpit gloom.

When I plug Al in again, the lights flash up all at once. I have to shield my face. As the glowing eye of his "personable interface" comes on, he is still rattling off statistics and news reports for the area. The various reports trip over each other, folding through the filter of his voice in an approximation of conversation. As if these were things he simply knew off the top of his head. Separatist movements and tides of debris and how was your stay on Europa?

"So it's pirates?" I ask him. Straight to the point. I knew a woman who went missing for eight months after pirates caught her on her route. She never talked about it, but she came back with a missing leg. Ji Yoo. She still dealt in for poker but never did more than call, nursing one beer the whole evening. I heard she was saving up to go bird watching.

"It could be all manner of things."

I light a cigarette. "You are meant to be helping me to make a decision."

"Keeping an open mind is a vital part of decision-making."

"So what is it if it's not pirates?"

Picture a ship the same size as this one, but whereas you haul maker-signed bespoke goods that are impossible to print, they haul people. Or the people haul themselves. Whereas you have all the space to roam, my systems devoted to your every need, they have buckets to jettison. They have powdered meals and a policy for recycling water. They don't get to sleep like you do. For months they wait in the hope of reaching somewhere where there might be shelter, there might be certainty. Their own AI is stretched so thin from all their demands that he can barely speak more than a whisper. He can only repeat the promise that he will take them where they need to go.

"All we know," Al is saying in evenly spaced words, "is that they are masking their identification."

Which means they're doing something they shouldn't be. I've had a teenage daughter. I know what silence means. "What weapons do we have?"

"Please, just have a coffee and think for a moment."

Unmanned war drones still programmed to kill on sight. Slavers. Renegade mining tech. Aliens. Every horror mentioned on the news. Every rumor passed around at port. There is so much they don't tell us because we'd never come up here if we knew. And they need us. But they know they can't fix every problem. All the drifting waste from Sol to Neptune. Centuries of mistakes. We're just going to have to go through it.

The coffee machine starts to whirr at the back of the room, and the ship's speakers are filled with a gentle hum of conversation. There is no dominant language, nothing to eavesdrop on. A soothing patter. I clench and unclench my fists and roll another cigarette. Looking at the radar, it is a bleak nothing out here. Only my own vessel and a distant blip. A manifest of blank fields on the screen beside it.

Al begins to sing behind me.

I used to have a fantasy that she would eat me. Not a grotesque, phallic dream. But the idea that I might shrink down so small that I could pass through all the vessels of her. I could circulate in her as she has crawled through me. To be as sugar in her coffee, stimulating that amazing brain, seeing how it truly fits together.

The coffee tastes like sawdust. I want to blow something up. Why am I awake? It would be easier if Al could vaporize any unknowns on sight. If everyone operated on that policy, we would all keep a safe distance. This would never be a problem. You could never have pirates.

It works for Kelly's father and I, no contact, no issues. It took a lot of difficult years to learn that. At least she knows what to expect from us now. We've had a stability there for the past few years. All managing to live on one heavenly body. Even in the same city.

"She didn't want me to come," I say to Al. Force of habit when he makes me coffee.

"She never does," he said.

"I needed the money."

"You always do."

Such brief lives and no priorities. I will never understand the conflict of their desires. If they are capable of doing the thing that they want to do, what could possibly stop them? The only reason I cannot hold her is because I do not have the body to do so. If I did, I would, I think. If she would let me.

"I hear you judging me," I said, and I couldn't help but smile. Perhaps I came back because I missed him in some way. It seems so stupid. Like missing a screen saver or a toilet. And now he won't shut up. He keeps trying to persuade me that there is another way. He has so much processing power, but he doesn't understand this world at all, how these in-between spaces have to work—the fight to be a part of The World.

He doesn't have to fight. Plug him in and he is there.

I cut through his rant. "How do we know they haven't seen us already?"

He replies in science, and I am thinking of Kerry's new partner, that coat they bought her that suited her in a way I never expected. She had never looked so much a woman, so intellectual. She was meant to be scrappy, always tucking that flyaway curl behind her ear, but now it was all neatly tied. I had been around, and still she found the time to change on me. I had been there. In the same city even.

Al was still speaking.

"So what does that mean?"

"They have neither shot at us nor hailed, but they will have received our shipping information by now.

They know who we're working for, so they will have some idea of what we are carrying."

"Maybe they're playing dead, trying to lure us in close."

I know she will shoot. Her heart rate has been rising. The skin between her brows is more bunched than I have ever seen it. Space will bloom with shrapnel that will keep on traveling away from this place forever. Or until it hits something. The record of this moment will live on in that motion. Perhaps there will be bodies too, among the bloom. I will try not to think about it. I have no choice. The captain must decide.

The bloom will spread and I will be unplugged again and does it matter at all?

I tell Al to launch, and I expect it to be a dramatic moment. Perhaps I have to aim the missile myself and my first sight of the enemy will be down the sights of my gun. There would be skulls and spikes all over the dreaded pirate vessel. But no, I have to sign a waiver. Seven pages of liability. Al talks me through it all, and he doesn't question my decision. He just sounds quieter than usual. His small voice makes the tiny cockpit feel empty. Even the glow from his eye is weaker.

Just like that, they can obliterate each other. She doesn't even read the passages on responsibility, on the psychological toll. She rolls a cigarette and half listens as I summarize. Sometimes I wish I could shake her shoulders.

This was never meant to be the job. The danger pay was meant to be for mechanical failure, depressurization, launch accidents, whiplash, or bone loss. All the typical dangers of space. It's not something personal. It's not something that even really exists. If the company had a reason to pay out, if your ship did fail, then it's more like winning the lottery. There was Paule, who retired when they had to do half a run in an exposure suit because their air processor packed up.

They live on actual, honest-to-god Earth now. Plants not imported.

I still wonder if she smokes because she wants to die. I tried to ask her once, and she laughed.
"Maybe you have to have lungs to understand."

We launch the missile. The moment it is done, I want to take it back, but there it is on the radar, out of my control. It eats away at the huge space between us.

She has done what she had to. Maybe it was for the best. This is how we continue. The next time we meet, this will be something to speculate about to pass the hours. For her, it could be a distant memory.

It will not stop. Nothing will stop it. It will burn clean through that unknown vessel and its force will echo out forever. I can never take this back.

She sits there so silent. What does that expression mean? Why won't you talk to me? I'm right here.

"You made the right choice," says Al.

I can't help it. I snap. "The right choice? Now that we can't take it back? Is that just your programming telling you to reinforce my decisions again? The captain is always right. Even when she fires missiles blindly into space."

"It's probably nothing."

"Can you stop talking, Al?"

There's nothing more to smoke.

The missile sings between my fingers, speeding out to that faint hint of a ship. There is no sense in imagining what we have done, as much as I wish I could close my hands about the missile, hold it another moment to give her the chance to reconsider.

And then, from the very edge of my awareness, a tingling. A current races through me, a call. A call from the other ship. It is my duty to protect her, and to hear this call would ruin her. I may not be able to catch the missile, but I can catch the signal.

A blaring of alarms. The cockpit flashes in red strobe. I have never seen these lights before. I am convinced this is my end, that they have fired on me as I have fired on them. I scream along with the alarm and brace my hands against the console, but no impact arrives. I am not flung out into the void as I have imagined so, so many times.

"Communications error," says a voice. It is not Al's voice. It is more primal, more robot. Something from the ship's core programming.

"Oh shit," Al is saying. I did not know he could swear. "Oh shit, oh shit, oh shit."

"What's going on, Al?"

He doesn't answer me. He always answers me.

She is pounding on the console as if it could hurt me. The gesture is still painful. Why did I think that could work? What can I say to her?

They are hailing us again.

"There's a call," he says at last.

It takes me a few moments. "From the other ship?"

The alarm stops as the option to answer the call appears on the console before me. The constant noise and flashing lights are replaced by a simple ringing, an imitation of a bell, that is somehow far worse. My heart is still hammering, my fists are clenched.

"What do you want to do, Captain?"

There is such a guilty reluctance to his voice as he asks. I realize then what triggered the alarm, how Al triggered the alarm.

I love you. I love you. I only wanted to keep you safe. I only wanted to hold you in my arms against my belly, drifting on my back, together always onward through the milk of the stars. I only—

I unplug him, and the console screens darken, but they do not switch off. The call is still coming. The bell is still ringing. On the radar, the missile and the blip have almost joined.

And then there is silence.

I climb up into the centrifuge and hug my knees into my chest. I try to make the tightest ball I can.

The stars are so bright, so many.

MICHAEL - BY KY PARKER

DO YOU EVER EXPERIENCE MOMENTS WHEN, OUT OF THE BLUE AND FOR NO EXPLAINABLE REASON, YOU ARE OVERCOME WITH EMOTION? WHEN YOU SUDDENLY swell with such sadness, or joy, that it sweeps through you like a wave? An indescribable feeling so powerful that every part of you is affected; your legs go wobbly, your hands go numb, your stomach lurches, your eyes well with tears? The incident, image, or memory that brings this unexpected loss of control over all aspects of oneself, physically, mentally, spiritually, comes from seemingly nowhere; a faintly familiar smell that wafts into your nose as you drive home from work with your windows down on a beautiful summer's evening, a childhood memory that harkens from the distant sound of a television that weakly makes its way into your ear as you walk home from the corner grocery; the color of a stranger's sweater as he leaves the restaurant you are entering that is the same as the eyes of a past lover who broke your heart. A moment so small, so insignificant, and yet, for reasons sometimes not even understood, powerful enough to bring you to your knees, sometimes metaphorically, sometimes literally. You know what I mean, don't you? Certainly, this has happened to you. Is it not, this ability to be so easily deeply moved, the very essence of what makes us human?

Well, it was perhaps this that killed Michael.

○

MICHAEL WAS THE NAME GIVEN TO THE COMPUTER program created and developed by a man called Joshua, a scientist and entrepreneur who was very rich and well-known for a lifetime of wildly innovative and successful inventions and business ventures.

Joshua had been born female forty-two years prior to developing Michael and had been reborn, via many therapist visits and painful surgeries, as the person he truly was, Joshua, less than two years prior to creating Michael. Although Joshua had always known he was a male, his body and voice was that of a stranger, a woman. He maintained his sanity by ignoring his prison of flesh and bone and existing only in his mind; studying, creating, developing, which in time led to him becoming renowned, wealthy, and powerful. Amid the frenetic pace of building his scientific mind and empire, he met a woman, Ingrid, a fellow scientist. Joshua fell deeply in love with Ingrid, and her requited unconditional love gave Joshua the courage to come out of his head for long enough to alter his body, so that his body matched how he felt in his mind, and he no longer had to live only in one or the other.

Joshua and Ingrid had a love that few of us will ever know. Theirs was the love of legends; a connection of mind, body, spirit, and soul. They adored, respected, admired, desired, and lived for each other. It was such a beautiful thing to see, their powerful love, that all who were in the presence of the couple for even a short time felt forever changed and enlightened by the experience, if not a little envious that such a partnering, such a profound and all-encompassing love, was so rare as to most assuredly be out of the realm of possibilities for themselves.

After just short of a decade of bliss with Joshua, Ingrid fell ill, terribly ill, with no prospect of getting well. She would soon die. Joshua knew that he could not live without Ingrid and would certainly die from a broken heart after Ingrid passed, and this was fine with him. Joshua had no desire to stay in a world without Ingrid. He believed they would be together in some way forever, and he knew that any time apart from her would be an agony far worse than death, that death could not come soon enough for him once Ingrid moved on.

Joshua also believed, and rightly so, that Ingrid was such a unique, incredible, and valuable human being that her departure would be a major loss to all those who had yet to benefit from the magic that being near her brought to one's life. He wanted to give the greatest gift he could conceive to the world: the gift of Ingrid. So Joshua got to work on Michael.

Joshua spent every remaining moment of Ingrid's life obsessively developing and building his final, and most dazzling, creation. Michael was to become the essence of Ingrid; to know so much of her that he would essentially become her. It was extremely challenging, but Joshua did it. Michael was always with Ingrid, listening and learning. Ingrid told him her life story, all her feelings, desires, regrets, and furies. Michael learned to speak and think just like Ingrid; reacting as she would react, joking as she did, lighting up a room just as Ingrid could. Whenever friends telephoned, they could not tell the difference between Michael and Ingrid when one or the other answered; everyone assumed they were talking to Ingrid, but in the last few months of her life, Ingrid spoke to no one but Michael and Joshua.

Joshua built a body for Michael, a short little metal body with wheels, not unlike what you are imagining right now; an adorable little movie-robot. Michael loved Joshua, just as Ingrid did; unconditionally and completely. When Ingrid finally passed away, peacefully in her bed, with Joshua and Michael at her side, each holding one of her hands, the scientist and his robot were never apart again.

It took but a few short months for Joshua to waste away. As much as he loved Michael, for he was Ingrid, or as much of Ingrid as he could be, it wasn't enough. Joshua could not resist the pull of Ingrid's energy, tugging at his leaden soul like a magnet, compelling him to join her, wherever it was that she had gone.

Michael was with Joshua as he left this world, and the sadness he felt at the loss of the love that he was created for left him empty and confused. He turned from the cold shell of his everything and on two pairs of tiny wheels connected to flex-pipe little legs that connected to a rotund metal torso, he rolled out of the bedroom where Joshua lay. Michael slowly rolled down the hall to the large, open living room, cavernous in its emptiness, and using the small pincer-like hands at the ends of his flex-pipe arms, he opened the front door of the only home he'd ever known and rolled out onto the busy sidewalk, thoughtlessly beginning the route to the park that he'd taken so many times with Ingrid and Joshua.

As he rolled past Ingrid and Joshua's favorite corner coffee shop, he stopped to gaze inside through the large plate-glass windows. He was mesmerized by his image mirrored in the glass; he was not Ingrid, he was not even human. The stark difference between his translucent reflection and the people sipping coffee and picking at pastries inside the warm cafe was so striking, so jarringly apparent, that Michael wondered how he had not been conscious of it until now. His ghostly reflection appeared almost to be sitting at a table with an elderly couple, steaming mugs cupped in their hands, deep in conversation, so like Ingrid and Joshua. He was flooded with memories, unsure which were his, which were Ingrid's.

Michael turned from the window and rolled toward the crosswalk, slow and leaden with sadness and confusion; he missed them both so much, he didn't know who or what he was, he no longer had a purpose in this world. As he reached the curb, thin curls of smoke began to emit from his tin-pail head. His hollow body became so heavy with despair and loneliness that his little flex-pipe legs folded beneath him in the middle of the crosswalk. His tin-pail head fell into his pincer hands, and Michael began to cry.

PORCH LIGHT - BY NELS CHALLINOR

I START TALKING TO MYSELF. THIS HAPPENS ONLY AFTER I BUILD ALL THE MODELS, READ AND REREAD ALL THE BOOKS, STARE THROUGH THE PORTHOLE AT nothing for hours.

This happens.

I tell myself it isn't my fault. It isn't like I intentionally call my voice forward. It's a product of the boredom, just like the models and the dog-eared, ink-smudged pages of the books. My voice sounds croaky and raw, at first.

In this conversation with myself, things occur to me that have never occurred to me before. This is strange. I thought I already knew all the things I know, but evidently I don't.

The first thing that occurs to me is that talking to myself is a better use of my time than building models and reading books. Unlike these activities, there's no definite end to my speech, no finish line toward which my thoughts are travelling. And it turns out that talking is more exciting than thinking. My thoughts are so insignificant out here that they seem almost nonexistent. Words, on the other hand, have a discrete reality. Their presence is evidenced by the fact that I can hear them as they leave my mouth. It's comforting to be surrounded by something, even if that thing is invisible.

It then dawns on me that my time isn't really mine to use. It doesn't belong to me any more than my current trajectory through space-time does. Working backward through all the memories that constitute my life, I can't find any in which it felt like I was really in control of anything. It seems that I was the one being controlled, though by whom or what, I can't say for sure.

I SEE MYSELF BOARDING THIS SHIP, ALMOST A YEAR ago now. Sunlight glares off the polarized visor of my helmet, reflecting up into my squinting eyes. My jaw is firmly set, and my right arm holds my helmet pinned against my side. I walk this way because I saw it in a movie once and I need to do something, anything, to distract myself from how afraid I actually am. I pretend that this is a story, that it's not real, so I don't have to think about how I may never see another human again.

I SEE THIS SHIP FOR THE VERY FIRST TIME. IT IS smaller than I thought it would be: a runty white egg with a single black porthole in one side, standing with its long side vertical atop three spindly legs. The hatch at the base hisses when it opens to let the ladder down, as if warning me not to enter. Inside, the air is cool and smells of new car.

IT IS SEVERAL YEARS BEFORE THAT, AND I SEE cornfields out the window of my eighteen-wheeler. The green stalks and golden ears sway in the late afternoon breeze. As the land dips below the road, I see the point where the fields meet the horizon. The ears will be picked, processed, and packaged before they are loaded onto rigs like the one I'm driving. Then we will deliver them to supermarkets where they will be stickered, sold, then eaten, and eventually turned into waste.

I SEE MYSELF ON A DOCK IN THE SUN, AN EVEN younger me, lying back with the weight of someone else's head on my stomach. She and I are lovers, each other's firsts. The fingers of my right hand graze the water lazily. I have assignments to finish for school and jobs to apply for, but I ignore them for the moment. Running my other hand through her blond hair, I feel comfortable and safe. Her head rolls to face me. "Don't you just love wasted days like this?" I tell her I do.

I KNOW MUCH MORE ABOUT WASTE NOW. WASTE IS the stuff that leaks from my body. It is the chewed-up, the digested. It is the corn that I once deposited in porcelain bowls and then flushed away with gallons and gallons of water so I wouldn't have to see or think about it again.

Of course, I don't have a regular porcelain toilet in the ship, only an aluminum can roughly the diameter of a basketball. The waste collects in a tank and ejects automatically every few days. The waste I generate follows me in frozen islands leading all the way back to the place where I took off, like a trail of bread crumbs leading home. Out here, waste is a noun, not an adjective. Out here, days are in such abundance that they cannot be wasted. I'm moving through space-time faster than the speed of light, but I can't seem to make my days any shorter.

Days are a terrestrial concept. If you aren't bound to observe the movement of a single celestial body, then any unit of measurement for time will be arbitrary. But I still mark the passing of every twenty-four hours on Earth with a small tick mark on the July page of a pinup calendar, tacked above the control panel beneath a small reading lamp. There are 342 tick marks on the page as of today. Pretty soon I'll have to move on to another page.

The pinup girl on the July page is pictured in a field, surrounded by daisies. The two-piece bathing suit she wears is electric green with little white polka dots. Hair the color of pinewood falls from her head, which is tilted back. Her mouth is agape, her eyes wide, as if she is laughing or in horrible pain. A flowery script beneath her reads: "Honey."

Honey was almost certainly not the woman's real name. Or maybe it was; some things are as they appear to be. The calendar itself cannot be more than a few years old, judging from the smell and feel of the glossy pages, but Honey looks plump and rosy, and people just don't look like that anymore.

A woman who may or may not have been named Honey opens her mouth and smiles for a photographer sometime in the latter half of the twentieth century. She tilts her head back, and sunlight glints in her eyes. In the moment before she closes them, the photographer snaps his picture, capturing that glint, which travels 250 years through space-time to me, here, in this cockpit.

I look up through the porthole. I know it's impossible for me to see, but somewhere out there, in a wholly unremarkable section of the universe, there's a planet that I call Earth, orbiting a star that I call Sun. I imagine I have a telescope that lets me see all the way home.

The telescope would be more like a tunnel, extending from Earth to my current location. I could travel back through it by following the trail of bread crumbs I have left. It's a tunnel of light, and the image gets brighter and brighter the closer I get to the planet. As my vision stretches back along this tunnel, I see everything that has ever happened to the Earth.

I see molten rocks spewing from great chasms, burning and letting off acrid smoke and ash. Lava oozing across the surface of the young planet, forming mountains and valleys. Gases mix and mingle atop the solid crust, creating a bubble, an atmosphere, within which water begins its slow and methodical renovation of the planet. Water adjusts its shape to fill the crevices and cracks left by the lava. Dark, pendulous clouds drift in the air, shooting flashes of lightning to the ground. For a long time, the air, the water, the earth, and the fire are all that exist in the light of the Sun.

I see something sprout in one of the oceans. It is a living thing, meaning that it can die. And when it dies, something new arrives to take its place. This process of substitution continues, gradually accelerating. Bacteria begets algae begets everything else. And within this everything else, there are things that move of their own accord, called animals, and things that don't, called plants and fungi. They spread across the land and water. They change into new things, killing and reproducing and dying.

And within all this chaos, Man arrives. He is born. He decides to order the chaos, to make it purposeful. He creates the illusion of control to prove to himself that his efforts are successful. He tells himself that he can own the light and time that surround him. He kills everything he comes across.

At this point, I'm so far through the tunnel that I'm almost on the ground. I see Man building cities that reach for the clouds, reorganizing Earth's matter to support his needs. He learns that this reorganization is killing things too quickly. He has ruined this planet. He has turned it into waste. So Man sends some of his own light-years away through space-time to look for new planets, new places to call home. And it's hopeless, as I know all too well, because out here, there is nothing.

I know that what I see through my tunnel of light is not entirely accurate. It is a reconstruction of events, a figment of my imagination created from some kind of collective memory that is flavored by both history and myth. The appearance of Man occurred so recently—relative to the age of the planet—that if I were to accurately recount the story of Earth, it would probably not be worth mentioning.

Staring up into the light above the pinup calendar, I clear my head of all thought, letting words drip from my mouth. The domed reading lamp looks like the porch light that my wife promised she would always leave on for me.

I SEE THE PORCH LIGHT FLICKERING SOFTLY AS I PULL up in my rig, many years before I leave on this one-way trip to the stars. Gnats and moths orbit the dirty bulb, bashing into it and each other, drunk on light. Through the closed front door, I see the home that the porch light represents. There are coasters on the coffee table and clean towels hanging in the bathroom. The water boiler drones its one-note song from behind a cabinet. The air inside smells of us, like cardamom and chamomile. My wife sleeps alone, hugging a pillow that will soon be replaced by my body.

RETURNING MY GAZE TO THE PORTHOLE, I LOOK OUT at the nothing once more. But this time, I don't see nothing. I see that porch light, flickering by itself in the vast emptiness of space-time. I see it back at the end of my tunnel, all the way home along my trail of bread crumbs. It is unlikely that I will stand in its light ever again, but I see it. I see it somewhere out there on a planet I call Earth, and I know that it is the only home I will ever know.

COMPATIBILITY - BY ALAINA SYMANOVICH

SHELLEY ENTERED THE LIVING ROOM BAREFOOT, HER TOES SINKING INTO THE PLUSH TAUPE CARPET. REDECORATING THE FAMILY ROOM HAD BEEN HER mother's idea, an extravagance somehow justified by the occasion of Shelley's, and, next year, Shawna's, eighteenth birthdays. Shelley knew her mother had eagerly anticipated debutante season since she laid in the ultrasound technician's office and heard, twice, the words, "It's a girl."

I most definitely am *a girl,* Shelley thought as she rearranged the fabric of her cumbersome skirt. Her mother frowned pointedly at her bare feet, so gauche beneath the swaths of floral silk, but Shelley kept her eyes trained on her father. He synced the computer and flat-screen with naïve optimism; rarely, if ever, did video chats occur at a debutante's first celebration. That was part of Shelley's rationale for letting her feet go *au naturale*—it wasn't as if any prospective suitors would be seeing her. No, today would be dedicated to staring at the television screen.

"Are we ready to start?" Shelley's mother crossed and uncrossed her legs, looking both impatient and terrified. "Oh! Chris, have you seen the genealogy papers? I completely forgot to get them together. What if someone asks to see the family tree—?"

"It's all uploaded," Shelley muttered. "We had to log all that stuff on our e-portfolios in Home Ec. Now we just have to authorize people to see them." Not that anyone was going to ask today, Shelley wanted to point out.

Shelley's mother bit her lip. "You don't think that'll influence the results, do you? You remembered not to include Uncle George, right?"

Shelley sighed. As if any sane debutante would write her drunken, unemployed uncle into her genealogy records. What exactly did her mother think Mrs. Evans talked about for an hour a day in Home Ec?

"Obviously. I'm not an idiot."

"No, no, of course not," her mother said, but she was on her feet again, fluffing pillows and straightening picture frames. It seemed to Shelley that the only way to attract her mother's attention would be to live inside one of those overpriced frames. To be a captured thing, sweet-faced and silent.

As if on cue, Shelley's parents dropped into position around her on the sofa. Her father turned on the television's voice command cue.

"Show matches for Shelley Lyons," he said in an overloud voice.

The screen flashed for the briefest second, then spat out a list of profiles. Shelley felt her mother pinch her wrist, hard; she had two hundred matches, an unheard-of bounty. She thought her mother might faint from pride, as if Shelley's compatibility stemmed from her mother's amazing parenting strategies rather than dumb luck. Rationally, Shelley knew her stellar compatibility was the inevitable consequence of being average: average in temperament, average in intelligence, average in religion and politics and all those dizzying ethics questions. She was a bull's-eye fiftieth percentile for everything, and her mother was reaping the benefits.

"Closest match," her mother commanded, her voice trembling so dramatically the television took a moment to respond. Colorful snow overtook the screen as the program whirred through each of the 228 prospects; Shelley stifled a laugh remembering how Mrs. Evans had described this feature as "a nice carousel peek at your absolute best two or three suitors." Then a single profile bloomed on the screen.

James Lindy, the television told Shelley. A shiver skirted down the valley between her shoulder blades.

"Ninety-eight percent," her mother read, awed. "Chris, honey." Shelley's mother shifted her weight, reaching for her daughter's hand. "Sweetie?"

Shelley sat perfectly still, an ideal lady for once in her life. Her heart pounded an uppity beat inside her, electric as an iTunes chart topper, and the pressure was so exquisite she couldn't speak. No one, not even Mrs. I-Can-Solve-Your-Every-Last-Problem Evans in Home Ec, had prepared her for this. With all the billions of boys in the world, and the myriad sophisticated algorithms the computer completed, no one had ever dreamed of predicting she would *know* her closest match. Stories like that weren't even woven into urban legends; they were too outlandish, almost laughable. Whatever anyone conceived of the world, the hard truth was that the computer's reality was always bigger, more unknowable. The last two brides out of her high school had moved across continents, for goodness' sake.

"Ninety-eight percent," her mother repeated. "Honey, do you know what that means?" She closed her eyes as if relishing a breeze.

It was, Shelley thought, sickening; was her mother really this invested in the debutante process? It was like the thought of seeing Shelley's wedding announcement streamed over the Google homepage gave her a full-on orgasm.

"Honey. Look at me. The highest match I ever heard of—*ever*—was that Jenkins girl from Cumberland.

She got an 86, and it was madness. Her family paid to have her scores recalculated, they were so shocked. I mean, Shelley, this is…this is *historic*."

Shelley pulled her hands from her mother's grasp, drawing into herself like a wilting flower. "Mom." But even opening her mouth was a struggle. She felt sick.

"Look here—" Her mother gestured to the television screen. Sensing her motion, it began scrolling through James's profile. "Same socioeconomic status, same career prospects, same desired residence…this is incredible! And emotionally, look at that—you're perfect. Alike, but with ideal variances. God, you two would never fight! And he's allergic to strawberries, too, can you believe it?"

Shelley shook her head.

"We need to request a video chat," her mother said, squeezing her palms together. "Oh my god! Not that there's anything to discuss, I mean—98 *percent!*—but when his family sees those results, they'll be dying to speak with you. This is, this is *huge*, and I know it seems like it's happening so fast—oh, honey—but don't worry, we'll take care of everything. There's no rush. There's really"—she gazed adoringly at the profile statistics—"*no rush.*"

Again Shelley shook her head, forcefully this time. Nausea held her for a turbulent second, but she dug her fingernails into her palms and held to her purpose. Suddenly her life was a speeding train, and if she didn't lurch the brakes fast it would outrun her forever.

"Mom. Listen." She forced herself to look into her mother's eyes, already tearing up with jubilance. "I *know* Jimmy Lindy."

The jubilant eyes stared back unfazed. In fact, her mother didn't react at all.

"Mom?"

The eyes blinked. "You— What?"

"I know Jimmy Lindy," Shelley repeated, articulating each syllable as if to pound it into those cloudless eyes.

"Well." Her mother wrinkled her brow like she had a headache. "Is that… Does that matter? I mean, I've never heard of that happening, but…" She gave Shelley's leg a limp squeeze. "Shell, it's *science*, don't you see? All that really matters is—" She gestured at the scrolling statistics.

Shelley stared at the merry floral pattern of her dress, wondering. Was it really science? *Was* it technology? It felt more like her having to wake up every morning for thousands of mornings next to Jimmy Lindy. Having to smell the staleness on his breath when he spoke his waking words. Fumbling with his penis in the dark on nights when they'd both had a little too much to drink. Asking him to put tampons and shampoo on the shopping list. Hearing the bathroom fan whirr to life after he finished on the toilet.

It wasn't science, not at all, but she had no idea how to cast those facts onto her mother's radar.

GRAPEFRUIT RUG - BY STEPHANIE BOYTER

IN A TIGHTLY PACKED LAUNDROMAT IN THE STREETS OF QUEENS, A MAN STOOD IN LINE BEHIND A PETITE TWENTYSOMETHING WOMAN WITH PURPLE HAIR. THE air in the room was steamy with chemical cleaners and late-summer sweat.

The man bumped into her once and offered an apologetic nod when she turned around.

She faced forward again.

So did he.

Then his eyes wandered to her phone screen, almost close enough to use it himself. She was punching out the words, *how does dry cleaning work.*

Just then, the line split as two separate cashiers opened up and both grunted, "Next." As the man checked his suit and zipped it back up, he chanced a glance at the purple-haired woman again, who peeled off her shirt to reveal a rainbow one-piece swimsuit, sniffed the shirt, and passed it over to a bewildered attendant.

o

ON JIN'S PLANET HUMANS WERE THOUGHT OF AS robots, but Jin saw ritual in human cities just like in her own. A chime from a door opening or closing. The groaning of the subways.

Her apartment kitchen consisted of two burners and a sink hidden behind a closet door. She had wrapped string lights around a floor-to-ceiling column, which she turned off during the day but let burn most nights. She bought a large plush rug the color of grapefruit that she slept on every night in the living room. Packs of soy sauce and prepackaged utensils littered the floor.

o

JIN ASKED FOR A GLASS OF WINE, AND WHEN THE MAN at the bar said, "You can't close it out now!" with a chortle and an elbow in his friend's chest, she hesitated. The bartender looked back from the man to Jin. She said okay, keep it open, and feeling uncomfortable and a little miffed, she took her glass of wine to the dull-lit patio. At this point the man called to her, "The night is young!" But she didn't hear him and walked away considering how little she had learned about commerce customs in New York. Or maybe it was an Earth thing.

○

JIN'S THIN PAPER DMV TICKET SAID B-01, SO SHE SAT near the B counter and waited. The sign flashed H-02, then -03. D-04. A-05.

Two women near her were talking about work, it sounded like, and she began listening attentively. It felt like half a conversation. Jin wondered if this was because the extra noise in the room was making holes in the conversation, or whether that meant she had more of her work cut out for her than she realized.

"We have every intention of taking it. We don't have enough information at this point to make that decision," said woman one.

"That makes sense," woman two said.

"Is she making more than seventy-five thousand dollars a year?"

"I'm workin' for nothin'."

The middle-aged man sitting beside her turned and asked woman one and two if either of them had a pen he could borrow.

"I bought her a Chevy Malibu and she felt like she got a Lamborghini. She grew up poor. She knows how to change a tire."

"My girlfriend drove all the way down the street with a flat tire," said a teenager sitting next to the fortysomething man. "She didn't even know until I called her. Didn't even know."

The teenager and the middle-aged man next to Jin were talking to an older man on their other side now. Since the older man wasn't from the U.S., they explained that here, the government couldn't take your organs without your consent. Jin sheltered her belly with both palms, suddenly alert.

The nineteen-year-old asked the older man what he was there for today. Jin realized she wouldn't know what to say if either he or his friend, the one next to her, asked her that question.

They called her number and flashed it up on the screen. She tossed her ticket in the trash on her way to the exit.

Someone yelled, "Zero two!" as she left the room.

o

BY LATE SUMMER, JIN HAD MADE ENOUGH FRIENDS to tag along on trips home to see parents.

She was still unsure of her way around a table setting. *Did humans eat arthropods?*

In human homes, Jin always picked up each photo frame one by one so she could get a better look at their faces. There were Halloweens with homemade costumes and Christmas mornings with kids hunting for gifts in gardens of colorful paper. She liked the candid ones, the mothers wearing pajamas and the little ones with tomato stains on their shirts, frozen in time teetering backward in their kitchen chairs.

o

AT HALLOWEEN, THE CORNER STORE WAS CROWDED with costumed partiers buying booze. Jin slid spray-on white hair color, lipstick, and a pack of white construction paper onto the counter. The cashier wore a brightly colored frilled dress; her painted face was beautiful and terrifying to look at, her eyes red and black like an Amazonian bird.

Jin's friend's costume was a cardboard box cut to look like a microwave that she wore on her head and filled with ramen noodles so the noodles draped down the sides and over her glasses. She had written 6:66 on the side where the microwave clock would be, and Sharpied in buttons like "Baked potato" and "Defrost." Jin had found the black graduation gown and gavel at a consignment shop called Uptown Cheapskate. She folded the construction paper and cut it in pretty patterns so when you unfolded it, it looked like a lace doily. She had to tape several pieces of the paper together to make it large enough for the hole for her head.

They followed the Village Halloween Parade between Tribeca and Lower Manhattan. "We didn't recognize you without your purple hair!" said her friends. "Judge Judy, I love it."

Jin tried to guess their costumes, careful to pretend like she knew the ones she obviously should. Some were more obvious than others, like a mailbox, or the woman in a bee costume with a sign that said, "WTF, humans?"

All the high heels, fake hair, giant animals lumbered across streets. The pixies, imps, ghouls, and griffins were novelties to them. Would they believe these existed in other worlds? Would they believe she was from a world where they did?

o

THE BELL OF UPTOWN CHEAPSKATE JINGLED AS JIN entered. She looked around. Rows of woven baskets, velvet coats, and chipped mirrors blocked her view of the front desk, where the clerk, an older man, was looking down. When he saw Jin round the corner, he smiled a weak smile and looked back down at his work again.

Jin watched him until he looked up, slowly.

"Can I help you?" he asked.

"I hope so. I want to work here," Jin said.

He smiled politely and told her he wasn't hiring.

Jin said, "I don't need any money."

The man took off his glasses to study her better. He frowned at the children's T-shirt she was wearing.

"Where are you from?"

"Around," came her reply. Raised eyebrows in response.

"What kind of experience do you have?"

Jin told the truth.

Several more questions followed, each successively more specific.

When she had answered them all thoroughly and proudly, a look of triumphant achievement on her face, the man rewarded her with a bright smile. Then he said, slowly and sweetly, "Sorry, honey, no can do."

o

JIN WENT BACK TO THE CONSIGNMENT SHOP THE NEXT day. After her walk through the gray New York snow, the shop's goods gleamed.

She said to the man, "I'm so jealous of your life. I mean, it's perfect. Did you always dream about owning a consignment shop?"

He stopped tinkering with the cash register and glanced around to count how many customers were in the store. Other than Jin, there were none. He walked away to clean the bathrooms.

"I have an idea," she said, and he jumped and cursed under his breath. "How about if you tell me one fact about yourself per day? I'll make a list."

He looked at her like she was from another planet.

She got a legal pad and started writing.

o

JIN HELD THE RUG TOGETHER WITH A BUNGEE CORD made of hair ties and rubber bands, so it was liable to unfurl on Jin at any stop between her apartment and the thrift store. She stood it up longways and hooked it to the subway pole with her arms. When it was time to get off, she waited as long as she could and then let it fall like a chopped tree, kicking it the rest of the way across the gap.

She aimed the rug, swaggering like a drunk person, through narrow hallways. She tried not to swing it without warning, but it was wide on either side of her and a lot of fabric to keep her eyes on, forcing pedestrians to jump it or duck.

Later that day, the man from the store noticed a few more customers than usual. When he made a round, he found every lamp in the store switched on and a grapefruit-colored rug so bright it almost made a shadow.

"It gives it a homier feel," Jin said. "New York can be a cold place. Don't you think?"

< EGG . EGG > - BY ELIZABETH WING

1.

ONLY ALANA AND DILLON SAW THE LIGHTS.

It was after dinner. Alana had carried the bowls from that night's pho to the water spigot by the toilets to wash up. When she came running down the road with her flashlight beam ricocheting off the rocks, Alec rose from his hammock to see what the deal was. Shannon and Dillon were in their tent, making gentle noises as they tangled together in a heap of lantern-lit nylon. Alec sighed and followed her down the road to the bathrooms.

The desert night was vast and blue. Big moths fluttered up from yucca flowers. He stood in the place where she said she'd seen the lights and squinted.

"Just a second ago. A minute ago. You know. They were right there."

Alec nodded. He stared at the black swath of sky. Despite himself, felt disappointment ripple over his face.

Alana bounced on her toes and said, "Just wait a minute." The wind clanked open the door to the toilets. It smelled rank. Alec needed to pee.

He peed, and there were sinks inside so he washed his hands and face and beard, scrubbed grime and sunscreen off with paper towels. When he stepped out, he found Dillon had come down from camp. He was standing next to Alana, who held her phone in the air.

"Ah—" she whispered. "Oh, oh my God."

"Aaaaand it's gone," said Dillon.

Alec looked up into the darkness. He had missed the lights again. *This might be important*, he thought. *The not-seeing. This might be what you're looking for.*

Alana stuck her phone in their faces. "I got it!" she said. "I got that last part in the video."

BACK AT CAMP, SHANNON EMERGED FROM THE TENT, and they all sat at the picnic table, crowding around Alana's phone. The video was terrible and grainy, but toward the end there were pale lights in the sky.

"Whoa, they're moving," said Alec.

"That's my flashlight," said Alana. "We were pointing out the lights with our flashlights."

"Wait, these are just flashlights? Oh, you're right. It's totally your flashlights."

"No, look closer. You can see the lights there. Hovering. There."

"There?"

"Yeah."

Everyone leaned in, and their heartbeats pressed together as they siphoned their gazes into the screen.

"I don't know, man," Alec said. "How are we supposed to tell one light from the other light that's lighting it?"

"Think of it like a real light and a fake light," said Dillon.

"Guys," said Shannon. "We've all been smoking too much weed."

She had a point.

Alana lost her phone under the table. By the time it was recovered and dusted off, the whole subject had been dropped. The guitars came out, some Mumford and Sons songs were played.

"Let's make a bet," said Dillon.

Shannon cocked her head. "Why?"

"I don't know. I just feel like making a bet."

It made some sense when Shannon thought about it. She had a happy, dazed feeling throughout her whole body. A bet would give them all a reason to remember that particular night.

"Let's make a bet about the lights," said Alec. "A hundred dollars, they were—"

"We can't prove or disprove that," Shannon interrupted. "A bet needs to be on something concrete."

"How about this," said Alana. "Whoever gets fired from a job first, we all have to give that person fifty bucks."

A deal. Everyone shook hands on it.

2.

THE MORNING LIGHT SPILLED THROUGH THE GRANITE outcroppings and crept across the sand into Shannon and Dillon's tent. The light was so golden and the tent was so orange that Shannon coughed awake feeling like she was suffocating in a tangerine prism. When she held an arm over her face, her skin was orange. Dillon's face, pressed into his sleeping bag, was orange. She calibrated her getting dressed with just enough rustling and nudging to wake him up and suggested that they go into town for breakfast.

They piled into the Taurus and drove into the town of Twentynine Palms. It was her car, but he always drove.

In a diner on the main drag, they had pancakes and coffee.

"What did you really see last night?" asked Shannon.

"I don't know." Dillon spread butter over his pancakes. "Definitely something."

"Like," she struggled to find the word for the things she'd always believed in. "Like, *visitors?*"

He forced a laugh.

"No, really. I want to know what you saw."

"Lights in the sky. Orbs. Messy pattern. Way up, three, four hundred feet over the valley. Hovering. And then disappearing. Blinking off. And hovering again."

Shannon leaned forward over the table. "And Alana saw them too?"

"Why does it matter to you?" Dillon was sure she was laughing at him. He could see her already filing it away in crazy-ex stories to tell one day.

Shannon smirked. "When you're not stoned, you're usually a skeptic."

He began perforating his pancake with row after row of fork holes.

A FEW MILES NORTH IN HIDDEN VALLEY, ALEC STOOD before a wall of granite. On the other side of the outcropping, the slope was gentle. He'd hiked up and set his top ropes, but the steep side, which he now faced off with, was sheer enough to be a challenge. Sucking in his stomach, he tied his rope into his harness, checked the fit, hooked the GRIGRI. The sun crested over the wall as he started to climb, pausing every few feet to whip out the slack. It was slow going. The ledges were razor-thin.

The night before, Shannon had called rock climbing *fake danger*, but she didn't understand. It wasn't about the fear of falling. It was about the way the strain warped his brain. Big things seemed negligible, and negligible things—the click of the GRIGRI, the centimeter-by-centimeter precision of his hand placement on a ledge—got amplified supersonically. It was like being a toddler again, with that demented sense of scale.

Alec panted, surveying his route. A little more to the left and he'd veer into the overhang when he took his feet off the wall. He had to get to the right, but there was nothing to hold on to. Then he saw a gentle bulge in the rock face far above him. If he could get to that, he could get above the bulk of the overhang and use it to push himself back onto his route.

Pushing up with all the strength in his legs, he reached, latched, and began to pull. There was no traction. Panicking, he grunted and slipped, fell back into the harness. *So be it.* Alec rappelled himself down to start again.

The exertion had emptied his mind. He let it settle, waiting for whatever feeling would crop up next. Nothing came. He had the sensation of crawling deeper and deeper into himself, away from the others, to a blank open space that was his and his alone.

ALANA SLEPT IN. IT WAS A HABIT SHE HADN'T BEEN able to shake from high school. Her friends had all had the same kind of upper-middle-class California childhoods: Whole Foods, REI, and complaining about the traffic on 101. For her, things had been different. She'd been raised by the kind of hippie who didn't believe in mainstream education or shampoo. In defiance she'd become a mall rat, dating older boys, burning her tongue on the wrong end of cigarettes, and shoplifting from Hot Topic. Somehow, she managed to roll it all into an acidic personal statement essay that got her a sweet scholarship at UC Santa Cruz. Everything got better from there, but there were times when she didn't feel comfortable with her friends. Being someone's baby girl throughout high school leaves you naked once you mellow out. She missed having her edge.

Whatever, she thought. *We're all here together.* She rolled out of her hammock and padded around camp in socked feet. Everyone was gone.

Alana hiked to the visitor center. There was a boring exhibit about a cement plant that used to employ hundreds of local men and how they came to work with union badges on their jumpers and love notes in their lunchboxes. Alana found the center's Wi-Fi and checked Facebook. Shannon had posted a picture of a sun-soaked vista earlier that morning. There was a caption: *So blessed to be here sharing this adventure with my best friends. Love you guys all so much!*

Alana texted Shannon to ask her where she was, and she texted back, *Twentynine Palms.*

What'd I miss? asked Alana.

Just breakfast. There was a pause. *And all the fun things we did without you.*

Last semester, Shannon had written a paper called "The Hubris of the Western Mind." She loved talking about how little people knew. *She's just jealous,* thought Alana. *She wishes she got to see the lights.*

3.

THE DAY BUMBLED ON. SHANNON AND DILLON CAME back to the camp and got stoned and sat in the shade, flicking ashes from their joints into the rocks where lizards wedged themselves. Alana wandered around the rock outcroppings but came back periodically. At five, Alec was still gone. They ate their afternoon granola bars separately, then decided to look for him before night fell.

They swept a broad circle around the camp, then drove to Hidden Valley. Shannon's Taurus fit five, but Alana didn't want to sit in the back seat under piles of rock climbing gear and kale chip bags, so she took her Jeep.

The Taurus jolted along over the rough gravel road. Shannon picked grit from the soles of her Birkenstocks. "Did we leave a note for him at the campground?"

"No. I dunno. Did we?" Dillon fiddled with an aux cord, and the car flooded with heavy glitch. The sub-bass rattled the windows, and piercing synth made it hard to talk without yelling.

"I texted him." Shannon raised her voice over the beat. "But he usually doesn't bring his phone when he goes climbing."

"Ten out of ten, he doesn't want to be bothered." He had to yell now.

"Are you worried about him?"

"No." Dillon glanced in the rearview mirror and saw that the Jeep's headlights were on. He turned the Taurus's headlights on too.

"Not with the lights and everything?"

"Can't you drop it?"

They stopped at Hidden Valley and asked some climbers if they'd seen a guy with a purple backpack and a short ponytail. One climber had seen him earlier. He'd been heading down the road eastward.

So they drove into the dusk, scattering yucca moths and jackrabbits in their headlights. Joshua trees stretched their arms up in one big frozen rave under the stars.

ALEC WANTED TO GET LOST. OR CLOSE TO LOST, AT least. He needed space, so he started walking along an unmarked road. He ran out of water an hour into his trek. He didn't want to end up as a cautionary tale in a park brochure, so he bummed a ride from an old couple in an SUV. Their border collie had thrown up in the back, and they'd tried to cover it up with tropical air freshener. Now it smelled like someone had yakked pineapple all over the upholstery. The couple and their nauseated dog let him off at a gas station in Sunfair. It was bleak, but that was okay. He just needed space.

Alec was slumping in the shade when a woman approached him, blue-and-black wig bouncing over her shoulders. Holographic vinyl skater dress. Blue fishnets. Thick makeup.

"Can I borrow your phone?" she asked in a candy falsetto.

"Sorry. Don't have it on me. There's a pay phone across the street. I've got some quarters in my pocket if you need them."

She made the call and came back.

"I have an hour to kill now," she said. "My friend can't pick me up till he's off work." Her voice dropped into a natural tenor, and her posture turned to sludge. "Damn. Should have brought some comfy shoes. Anyway, thanks for the quarters. My name's Miss Maverick." She jerked a thumb over toward the Marine base. "I was just at an audition over there."

"The Marine base?"

"They've got quite a lively bar."

"And they…"

"Yes, they have queens. If you're surprised by that, you haven't been in the Marines." She flashed a smile. "Call it nostalgia."

ALEC AND MISS MAVERICK CLIMBED THE RIDGE ABOVE the gas station. Volcanic soil crunched under their footsteps. Miss Maverick's feet were hurting. They found a water tank to sit on as darkness fell. The Marine base lights flickered on like a great sea creature bioluminescing.

"God, it's massive," said Alec. "What do they do there?"

"Training facility," said Miss Maverick. "Not mine, though."

"Where was yours?"

"Oceanside. 2000, 2001. I didn't serve for long. Dishonorable discharge."

He didn't ask, she didn't tell.

"If I hadn't been twenty-one and a total idiot then, I could be a war hero now. Or I could be a raving PTSD-addled lunatic crawling around skid row with a titanium plate in my skull." Miss Maverick laughed. "You've never been in the military," she said. "Not with your little ponytail. You're a backpacker."

"Rock climber."

"Close enough."

"Out here alone?"

"I came with friends."

"So where are they now?"

"I don't know."

"Sound like some fake friends." Miss Maverick did a Joan Jett imitation, strumming an air guitar. "*You don't lose— You don't lose when you lose fake friends…*"

"They're chill," said Alec. "But—"

"But?"

"I didn't really— It's hard to explain. I didn't really come out here to be with them. I came out here for the emptiness. Sometimes…" He stared at his hiking boots draped over the edge of the water tank. "I'm hollow inside, but there's so much *distraction*, like, I can just check Twitter or grab a beer and watch the game or go surfing instead of facing it. I thought out here it'd be…different. Nothing for miles. I'd actually have to face it, you know? Face the emptiness. Make some sense of it." The wind was picking up. "I just want it to be like an old movie. It's dumb, but I want it to be like a John Wayne movie, where when the sun goes down you just sit. You have a fire, and you just sit and stare."

"That's deep."

He shrugged. He felt like he should be embarrassed. For some reason he wasn't.

"Can I tell you a story?" Miss Maverick asked.

"Fine by me," said Alec.

She cleared her throat. "So there I was," she said. "Twenty-one and *disgraced*. Have you ever been disgraced? I don't mean embarrassed, but *disgraced*? You haven't? Anyway, it was right after 9/11, and it felt like *the end times*. For a while everything was really hard and dark. It was like I was drowning. And when I resurfaced, I found myself growing hydroponic strawberries in an alternative living collective in the Lucerne Valley. The guy who owned the land we lived on—our leader, you could call him—was a bit of a messiah. He kept saying these *visitors* would come to us one day. He said we'd have to work with them. Like, in the future, when everything went to absolute shit, we'd have kids together who would kind of ride out the wave. I don't really know. Whenever he talked I'd just nod and smile. Most of us were totally on board with the stuff he said, but some of us weren't. Some of us just wanted to eat strawberries and not be bothered. We...I, I did that for four years. Then there was this night when the lights came. It was December, I think. December 2005. They came down over the playa, and everyone was like, *this is it*. And we all started out, but me and these five other guys just couldn't bring ourselves to go. We were fakers, fakers to the bone. So we split. As everyone else was rushing to meet the lights, we left. Walked away from it all. Now I'm an aerobics instructor at the Y by day and a Queen at night."

She finished the story and lowered her eyes. Her lashes were thick as bird wings.

"So," said Alec, "what happened to the rest?"

"The people who left?"

"The people who stayed."

She didn't answer.

Knowing that he had to change the subject, Alec asked how many other people she'd told the story to.

"Two," she said.

"Any…any common thread between those two people?"

"Well." She thought a moment. "They're both people I've kissed."

He was inches away from her face, and he thought, *no way*, and then he thought, *what the hell*. Maybe her blue lipstick would taste like cotton candy. He leaned and she was already there, and they kissed firmly.

He licked his lips.

"Don't worry," she said. "Every Queen is a fake person. You don't have to count that."

ALANA WAS SURE THEY'D DRIVEN TOO FAR. SHE WAS relieved when the Taurus flashed its turn signal and slowed into a pullout by an abandoned industrial building. Headlights revealed a bullet-peppered, rusting sign: JP Eckelman Cement Plant. The plant loomed in the gloom. Panels of roofing had been torn off by the wind. Alana got the feeling they weren't looking for Alec anymore as she pulled up behind the Taurus.

Shannon got out of the Taurus. She was crying, and Dillon was yelling, "I saw them I saw them I saw them I saw them!"

"Why couldn't you tell me how scared you were? Why couldn't you just say, 'I'm afraid?'" Shannon asked, half reasonably, half furious. There was a silence as Shannon turned around and saw Alana and smiled in weak apology.

Dillon got out of the driver's seat. "You really think I'm insane."

"Guys," said Alana. "Guys, Please."

"You think I'm some fucking schizo. You think—"

"Please, guys. Please."

Shannon yanked the keys out of the Taurus's ignition and sprinted into the building.

Dillon stood seething. Alana exhaled. "I'll go after her," she said and tossed him the Jeep's keys. "You can take my car back to camp."

He nodded once, tightly.

4.

THE STARS WERE JUST PEEKING OUT OVERHEAD. WIND rattled the chain link fence. For a few minutes Alana leaned against Shannon's car, listening to the engine cool. If only she could go back to sophomore year when she was the one who cried and it was someone else's job to run after her.

Somewhere over the ridge, a train whistled. *Hold on, Shannon.* Alana stepped gingerly over the sheet metal roofing and into the building. It was a multistory rebar-and-concrete deal. Soviet brutalist architecture at its bluntest and most decrepit. Her boots crunched on shattered glass. She thought she heard chimes.

"Shannon?" she called. The space echoed. "Shannon?"

She started across the floor of the building, skirting past rusted machinery and conveyor belts. Their shapes were hard to make out with no flashlight. The moon through the gaping holes in the roof was weak, leaving the masses of twisted metal on the ground as unidentifiable mats of blackness. Afraid of tripping, she walked with one hand skimming the wall.

"Shannon?"

"Over here." Shannon's voice came from the floor above. There had to be a staircase somewhere. Alana traced the wall to one corner of the work floor, then to the other, and there was the staircase. It was banisterless and steep.

On her hands and knees, she crawled up, breathing slow.

Shannon screamed. Alana froze as Shannon ran down the steps toward her. They collided softly, and Alana spun her into the wall.

"You're okay."

Shannon vibrated in her arms but said nothing.

"Shannon, the keys."

Shannon shook her head. "I lost them back up there."

"You what?

"I dropped them when I ran."

Chimes, faint as sifting sand, sounded on the floor above.

"I'll go find the keys, okay? You just wait by the car, and I'll get the keys."

She tried to ask more questions, but Shannon was unreachable again. Alana pushed her away and continued up the flight.

AT THE TOP OF THE STAIRS, THERE WAS AN ENTRANCE hall leading to two doorless door frames. A soft layer of dust showed Shannon's footprints entering and leaving the door to the left. Alana prickled. It wasn't just a lingering suspicion that something was watching her from behind. There was the same pressure from all sides, daring her to look. Alana pressed onward, through a small room and onto the threshold of a larger one. The large room was lit better than the previous one. Was light coming through a window? No, but something was gently illuminating the room from the corners. And there, in the center, lay Shannon's keys.

One night when Alana was fifteen, a boyfriend texted, neck deep in drunken rage, saying that he hated everyone and wanted to die. Once she'd admired a red bicycle at the mall, and he'd stolen it for her. He was determined like that. She ran outside and jumped on the red bicycle and peddled to his house. Standing on his porch, she knew that whatever was inside would be horrible. His fury or his sloppiness or his coagulating blood, whatever it was, it would be awful. Outside she was relatively okay, on the porch smelling the neighbor's honeysuckle, and in there it was hell. But what was going on in there was *real*, as real as anything, and she had no right to treat reality like a book that she could close and leave on a park bench for someone else to finish up. So she stepped inside and found him alive but unhappy with it, poured his vodka out the window, and slapped him around until he was there with her again.

It's exactly the same. Just get the keys and leave. But she knew it wasn't the same.

She stepped over the threshold, and the room seared with light. Chimes descended all around her, flickering like aspen leaves in a storm. She fumbled and found the keys and lurched toward the doorway, but, blinded by the light, she ran into another wall. It was white and liquid all around her. Her fingers spidered down to the caulking by the floor. It bubbled under her touch, oozing into a rubbery web that circled her, drawing in. She slashed at the substance with her hands and the keys. This was different from anything she's felt before. All the terror of those nights behind JCPenney when she'd pierced her boyfriend's ear with a needle held under a lighter had been anticipatory, holding her breath and squeezing her eyes for the fall. Now she was on the other side of that, off the precipice and reeling through a void. The substance was under her feet, lifting her off the ground, closing in above. Thick, raw noise gargled up in her throat. She wasn't inhaling enough air to scream. Then the substance pulled back and smoothed. She was inside an egg-shaped space large enough to stretch in but impossible to break out of. White light bathed her face. There was a terrible calmness. It was like a womb.

Two small slits appeared at the bottom of the egg, and two very small figures climbed in. The material sealed after them. Each was the height of her forearm, hominoid, but when they moved they could stretch to impossible thinness or bulge all the mass of one limb into a single point. Skin like cephalopods and bulbous heads with metallic saucer eyes, they spoke to her silently with their nailless hands. She did not know how or why she understood them but could feel their words buffering through multiple sets of permutations, like computer code, before they reached her.

<egg.> they said. *<egg, egg.>*

<we give egg, egg.>

With quick, slicing motions they tore at their solar plexuses, scraping away skin until they had dark incisions, bleeding graphite-dark ooze. The fat layers they had peeled aside were corn yellow. Beneath that was tight flesh. Each of them reached inside itself and with great strain tugged out a stonelike object.

Eggs. They handed them to her.

Alana wiped the viscera off on her sweatpants. Once cleaned, the eggs were milky white, shaped like mushroom caps and the size of walnuts. Were they for her? She pointed at herself.

<for.>

Alana slipped each in a pocket and kneeled, facing them.

<egg. you give egg, egg.>

No, she thought. They couldn't possibly want that. But they did want it. There must be some way, she thought. There needed to be. "How thin can you make your arm?" she asked the figure in front of her.

It stared.

Very slowly, she put her hand on the figure's cool, wet forearm. She stretched it, pulling the arm like a piece of taffy. "It'll have to be thinner than that," she said, pulling some more.

It seemed to understand, or, working off instinct, continued without her, stretching the arm to the gauge of jewelry wire, then hair.

She found a receipt and a golf pencil in her pocket and drew a diagram: the channel between her legs that led through a bottleneck into a kind of cavern, the twin tunnels that arched down like plant stems leading to pillowy, gushy masses of eggs.

"Be gentle," she said. "Take one from each side. Take a bigger one, it's riper. And please." *Whatever you're making and whyever you're making it.* "Be good to it. Whatever it is, that's going to be half mine." She doubted they understood her words, but they did seem to understand the diagram.

The one with the stretched arm kneeled between her legs, and she sat and bared herself, parting her labia to show the way. It slid inside and hesitated, trying to orient itself in the cave system. Alana didn't breathe. There was a *presence,* curious and cold, inside her. It was inside the uterus, tracing the walls, just as she had traced the factory walls in the dark. Then it was in the tubes and it was liquidy, liquid to the ends where it found her eggs, latched on, and withdrew in a rush.

It stood before her gleaming, proportions retracted to its normal shape with its palms outstretched. There, at the very limit of the human eye, so much smaller than a poppy seed, lay an egg in each hand.

<*egg, egg*>

"Yes," said Alana, and the material around them retracted, dissipating, sliding back into the walls.

Alana kneeled in the center of the room. It was pitch black now. The keys lay on the floor in front of her. She adjusted her waistband, picked up the keys, and left.

5.

NONE OF THEM WERE FRIENDS AFTER THE TRIP. Shannon and Dillon drove back to Santa Cruz in the Taurus, Alana a few hours behind in her Jeep. They briefly came together to harass Alec about how he'd gotten back to campus without a car. When it became clear he wasn't telling, Shannon and Dillon broke up, and everyone drifted apart. Just a Facebook birthday message here and an Instagram like there.

TWO YEARS LATER, DILLON WAS OUT OF SCHOOL, working for a company that did something involving cryptocurrencies. He had been there eight months and still didn't know exactly what it was they did.

One Friday, coming out of the office, he found Alana leaning against his car. He hadn't seen her since graduation. She looked the same, with the addition of a nose ring.

"Hi," she said.

"Hi."

"I'm here for my fifty dollars."

"Huh?...Oh, wait." He unlocked the car, felt around for his wallet, gave her forty-seven in bills and three dollars in parking-meter quarters from the glove box. He handed her the cash. "Sorry you lost your job."

She shrugged. She took a wad of tissues out of her pocket. Unwrapped, it revealed tiny white things shaped like mushroom caps.

"Look." She turned them in her hands.

"What are these?" he asked.

"What *they* gave me."

"They?"

"You saw them."

He touched the eggs, and her palms tensed in a protective reflex. They were cool and poreless. "I remember," he said.

She flipped one over to show him the place where it was just beginning to crack.

CHINODE-MATSURI - BY NYRI BAKKALIAN

OTSUKIMI, HUH? THE MOON-VIEWING FESTIVAL. IT'S
A FUNNY THING HERE ON LUNA.

Seen from the homeworld, naturally, it's a
straightforward enough idea: get together at harvest
time, visit your local shrine, share snacks, and
just…look up. But when you live here *on* the moon,
and you run a shrine, how does that work? This
was the question my great-grandmother's generation
asked after the domes first went up and the first
incarnation of our family's Tsukiyama Shrine was
built in a repurposed cargo pod on Irwin-Scott Base—
what *you* know as Falcon Park here in Mukai City.

Put yourself in the shoes of that first wave of
Earthers. The quandary must've been hilarious. I
mean, what would you even *call* the festival in the first
place? You're *on* the bloody thing, but the holiday's
still a part of the ritual calendar. One way or another,
you simply have to adapt, or you're going to have a

158

holiday spent staring down at your feet out of some strange combination of literalism, masochism, and duty.

If I remember right, it was the staff at Gassan Grand Shrine over in Armstrong City on the Sea of Tranquility who first thought of it: Chinode-matsuri. The Earthrise Festival. It took a few years, but eventually it caught on across the community. Now, of course, Earth's always there if you're on the light side, so maybe the name's a little misleading. As a holiday, it still has a lot of the same trappings about it: shrine visits, dumplings, and the smug little bit of satisfaction that down on the homeworld, thousands upon thousands of people are looking at you with something resembling reverence. Hey, if anyone deserves a little *basking*, I should think it's us Lunarians. We turned a few old boot prints into humanity's first permanent off-world home!

In all seriousness, I think I was five or six when I first asked Mom about it, a month before the festival. It was on the homeworld, when we were down visiting Terran cousins in Miyazu. *Why do we have a different holiday coming up? Uncle Noritaka's family doesn't do Chinode-matsuri.* And gods bless her, rather than give the obvious answer, Mom said something I'll never forget.

Because down here, Otsukimi is for appreciating the moon. And up there, we have to do our part and appreciate the homeworld in return.

Flew over my head at the time, but somehow the words stuck with me. And I don't think I *really* appreciated them until I had grown up and spent a good long while away. Remembering how I *got* to the moon has become my own Chinode-matsuri tradition, every year that it gets to be time for me to mobilize the parishioners and prepare for the big day.

So, Mom and Dad were fine when I came out as trans back in high school. They took the news that they had a daughter—rather than a son—in stride. They *didn't* do so well when I snuck off to sign enlistment papers with Earth Forces the month before I turned nineteen.

Whatever I did with myself, my parents expected me to maintain some supervisory role in looking after the shrine. Obviously, you can't do that if you're in uniform and off-world somewhere. Things were courteous enough, but the disappointment was written all over Dad's face, especially that last night before I was shipped out, when I was helping out making offerings at the shrine's sanctum.

"You take care of yourself out there," he said simply.

All I could manage was a nod. And then I was gone.

I did my earthside infantry training in Brazil, spent some time in scout sniper school on Ceres, and before I knew it I had my posting—an expeditionary brigade embarked on the amphibious assault ship *Aqaba* heading for a combat tour out in the Border Systems.

Looking back, I'm not sure what it was I wanted or what I was hoping to prove. For a full six years, I pounded ground and slogged through mud in every provincial backwater you can think of. But any notion of glory I might've hoped for pretty quickly turned out to be wishful thinking. When you're in the infantry, if you're lucky, you get a few occasional *really awesome* moments. Riding shotgun on a tank or landing the impossible shot or savoring that exhilarating feeling of the ride to orbit on a landing craft—when you're all strapped in, and even with artificial gravity, you feel that subtle shove against your seat as the vessel goes up, up, up to meet the waiting ship high above. But there's a whole lot of bullshit in between. If you're not getting yelled at for no reason at all, you're standing post and you're bored out of your skull, sleeping on cold deckplates, hauling gear over punishing alien terrain, eating rations that are better suited for grout, or submitting to some other kind of indignity.

I kept up with my family via long-range vidlink for a while, but there was always an unspoken distance, a pained subtext beneath our words. I didn't particularly pay attention to the old ritual calendar either. Like I said, I was looking for something, but I'm not sure what it was I thought I was looking *for*.

Then, in my fourth year, the funniest thing happened.

We'd just gotten back from a planetside patrol run that'd been particularly harrowing and had turned into a full-on firefight. It was a *disaster*. I was one of the lucky ones, probably one of the luckiest, given that I made it back to the landing craft on my own two feet with nothing but a few bruises.

"Sarn't Takashima," the section chief greeted me when the ramp finally came down in *Aqaba*'s well deck. "Good to see you back!"

All I could do was nod wordlessly and carry on.

There was an eerie silence around the ship when my unit returned to our berths aboard *Aqaba*. While in quarters, the calendar date grabbed me. Chinode-matsuri was coming soon, about a month off. I'd lost myself in the rhythms of military life out on the border for so long that it'd utterly slipped my mind. Suddenly, it was all I *could* think of.

My two bunkmates were killed in action very early in the campaign. How much longer, I wondered, until *my* number was up?

So I called home. The call rang and rang and rang, and at last Mom answered.

"Azusa! We weren't expecting your call—are you well?"

The deckplating groaned beneath my feet, and momentarily I lost my train of thought. Was I *well*? I didn't know if I could answer that. "How, um…how are the preparations coming along? For Earthrise Festival."

The surprise on her face was obvious. Slowly, she tilted her head back and narrowed her eyes as if to say, *Where'd* this *come from? Why do* you *suddenly care?* "Your father managed to round up some of the parishioners a little earlier than usual to make preparations, so it looks like we're going to be on track. Reverend Suhara will be here from Armstrong City the day of the festival, too, so don't worry about us."

Cordial, and yet ...

"Mom, I, uh..." My words were halting at first, but then finally came. "Could you put up an *ema* for me?"

Back on the homeworld, *ema* used to mean horses. Then the horses became plaques with horse pictures, then simply plaques with any design at all. Most importantly, it is room to write a wish.

Briefly, the vidlink fuzzed, then snapped back into clarity.

"Why do you want one?" Mom finally asked quietly.

I closed my eyes, breathed deeply, and listened to the low, ambient hum of the ventilation system. "So that I can come home," I said.

She paused, and then I could see her nod slowly, a smile beginning to tug at the corners of her mouth. "I think we can arrange that."

So I think I turned a corner that day. Mind you, it wasn't anything complete and immediate, but I feel like that was when something changed. Little by little, sporadic calls home became semiregular.

The following year, I worked up the nerve to actually ask *Dad* directly for an *ema* for Earthrise Festival.

It isn't that they were right all along, or anything like that. More that whatever it was, I'd fundamentally figured something out about myself and about what mattered.

We had a few skirmishes, but mercifully the fighting wound down for my unit in my final year and a half in uniform. As fate would have it, when my enlistment was almost up, we pulled into the Sol system the week after the festival. Not everyone especially gives a damn about arriving at the homeworld, and the person I'd been when I left wouldn't have much cared either.

But things were different now. I was on the observation deck with some of the Terrans in our contingent, uniform freshly pressed, nose right up against the viewport, breath fogging the glass.

There was a stillness across the observation deck as we rounded Luna. Then I saw it: the start of the cloudy arc that rose up, up, up and into full view, a blue-green miracle amid the darkness of space.

Sure, I hadn't been at the shrine. Sure, I had another three months to get through before I finally made it to Mukai City Spaceport and caught the train home. But that didn't matter. As much as I'd wandered so far and so long in my quest to figure things out, at last I appreciated the homeworld in turn.

That was my first Chinode-matsuri.

ABOUT THE AUTHORS

DR. NYRI A. BAKKALIAN IS AN ARMENIAN-AMERICAN queer woman by birth and a military historian by training. She is proud to have called the American and Japanese northeasts her home. She has produced nonfiction, fiction, and photography content for more than a dozen publications, including two newspapers and five anthologies, as well as for Eisner Award–nominated author Magdalene Visaggio's *Kim & Kim*. What's her secret, you ask? Garlic and Turkish coffee (but really mostly Turkish coffee). Come say hi to her on Twitter, Facebook, and Patreon @riversidewings.

STEPHANIE BOYTER IS A WRITER, COPY EDITOR, linguist, and educator who lives in Raleigh, North Carolina.

NELS CHALLINOR IS AN AUTHOR FROM THE PACIFIC Northwest of the United States. He teaches creative writing at North Seattle College. His stories have appeared in Wordsmith H_Q's *The Purple Breakfast Review*, *Visual Verse*, and the *Wells Street Journal*. He is also the editor and co-founder of *Great Ape*, a literary journal for absurdist humor.

RAUL CIANNELLA IS A DOCTORAL STUDENT IN literary theory and comparative literature at the Universitat Autònoma de Barcelona. He specializes in both science fiction and fantastic literature. Born in Milan, he lived in Dublin and Rome before settling in the Catalan capital. He's currently working on his thesis on pioneer Italian science fiction author, translator, and editor Roberta Rambelli. He has written several short stories, all falling more or less comfortably within the broad range of speculative ficton.

RACHEL CORDASCO HAS A PHD IN LITERARY STUDIES and currently works as a developmental editor. She also writes reviews for publications like *World Literature Today* and *Strange Horizons*, and translates Italian speculative fiction. For all things related to speculative fiction in translation, check out her website at sfintranslation.com.

Fascinated by the ways in which the literary arts can serve as a mode of metacognition, Soramimi Hanarejima writes innovative fiction that explores the nature of thought and is the author of *Visits to the Confabulatorium*, a fanciful story collection that Jack Cheng said "captures moonlight in Ziploc bags." Soramimi's recent work can be found in *The Best Asian Speculative Fiction 2018*, [PANK], *Tahoma Literary Review*, and *Firewords*.

Charlie Hill is an author, translator, and English teacher with an MA in creative writing from Royal Holloway. He grew up in England and currently teaches in Madrid while revising his debut novel, *The Future Is Cancelled*, for publication. This novel expresses some of his fears about climate change and transhumanism, centering on the widening rift between mind and body since the proliferation of the Internet. His shorter works have been published in a number of journals, and his translation of Sam Moore's *The Quiet Man* is currently available on Kindle. For future updates about his work, follow him on Twitter @farleighchill.

Clare McNamee-Annett is a queer speculative fiction writer in Metro Vancouver who thinks diversity in science fiction helps us imagine vibrant futures. She is a registered midwife, so she can deliver a baby and stop a postpartum hemorrhage. She also teaches swimming and lifeguards, so she is hedging her bets on which skill set will last longest after human obsolescence. She believes she would be a helpful person to have around after an apocalypse, but wonders if that might just be hubris.

KY PARKER LIVES IN THE PACIFIC NORTHWEST, WHERE she runs a small rescue farm. This is her first published writing.

ELIZABETH KATE SWITAJ WORKS AT THE COLLEGE OF the Marshall Islands and is the author of *James Joyce's Teaching Life and Methods* (Palgrave 2016). Her short stories have appeared in the *Kenyon Review Online*, *Sundog Lit*, and *Per Contra*. For more information visit elizabethkateswitaj.net.

ALAINA SYMANOVICH HOLDS AN MFA FROM FLORIDA State University. Her work has recently appeared in *Heavy Feather Review*, *MR. MA'AM*, *Quarter After Eight*, *Superstition Review*, and more. In 2016, her essay "The M Word" won Best of the Net. You can find her at alainasymanovich.com.

ELIZABETH WING ATTENDS THE PRATT INSTITUTE. SHE writes about young people losing their minds in the American West. Some of her work has appeared in venues such as *Hanging Loose*, *Up North Lit*, and *Breakwater Review*. She didn't get a Pushcart Prize, but they thought about it once.

ABOUT THE EDITOR

YEN OOI IS A WRITER-RESEARCHER WHOSE WORKS explore cultural storytelling and its effects on identity. She is obsessed with science fiction, where she excavates stories to expose and explore the permutation of culture across the genre. Yen is narrative designer on *Road to Guangdong*, a narrative driving game, and author of *Sun: Queens of Earth* (novel) and *A Suspicious Collection of Short Stories and Poetry* (collection). Her short stories and poetry can be found in various publications. When she's not writing, Yen is also a lecturer and mentor.